The Terrible Fours

Ishmael Reed

The Terrible Fours

Baraka
Books

Montréal

© Ishmael Reed, 2021

ISBN 978-1-77186-243-1 pbk; 978-1-77186-244-8 epub;
978-1-77186-245-5 pdf

Cover illustration: Evany Zirul
Cover design: Richard Carreau Design
Book Design by Folio infographie
Illustrations: Ishmael Reed
Editing and proofreading: Blossom Thom, Carla Blank, Robin Philpot

Legal Deposit, 2nd quarter 2021

Bibliothèque et Archives nationales du Québec
Library and Archives Canada

Published by Baraka Books of Montreal
6977, rue Lacroix
Montréal, Québec H4E 2V4
Telephone: 514 808-8504
info@barakabooks.com

Trade Distribution & Returns Canada – UTP Distribution:
UTPdistribution.com

United States Independent Publishers Group: IPGbook.com

Dedicated to Ted and Lois Cunningham

Contents

Untangling "The Terribles"

The Terrible Twos, published in 1982, opened with a warning about the climate crisis:

> *By Christmas, 1980, the earth had had enough and was beginning to send out hints. Volcanoes roared. Fish drank nitrates and sulfur. A pandemic of sleepiness and drowsiness was sweeping the earth and scientists didn't know what to make of it. Some said that it was the coldest Christmas in memory as minus-40-degree temperatures blew down from the Arctic. Greece was struck with the worst snow blizzard in thirty years, The Times reported. "Wolves entered towns and villages to attack livestock." Declared Prime Minister Constantine, "Greece is not equipped to meet this sort of weather." In Italy, people were fleeing Naples. The Northern Hemisphere wasn't as much fun as it used to be."*

The Terrible Twos predicted the fall of the Soviet Union and pointed to the city where it would begin. Riga, Latvia. The CIA's director at the time, Robert Gates, said he didn't have a clue that this would happen:

Snow Man looked down at the newspaper as he took in mouthful after mouthful. There had been huge headlines for weeks. The Soviet Union was putting down rebellions in Estonia, Latvia, and the Ukraine. The rebellions that had begun in Riga had spread.

Vice President Dean Clift ascended to the presidency after the death of 91-year-old General Scott, the hero of Dominica. It was Wall Street backing that got Clift elected on the basis of his good looks. Clift was a high fashion model whose photos graced the pages of leading fashion magazines. Champagne and cocaine were passed around on Wall Street because now they could use Clift to cut taxes, eliminate regulations, starve the poor, develop the wilderness, pollute the air, and police the uteruses of millions of women. Erase the gains of the Civil Rights movement. Eliminate a variety of polyamorous relationships. Clift played ball with his sponsors until a tragic event. His wife, the First Lady and his anchor, Elizabeth, insisted that a tree deemed sacred by Native Americans be used as the White House Christmas tree. As she lit the tree she was electrocuted. Clift sank into a deep funk. But then, during his dark night of the soul, St. Nicholas guided him through the underworld where former politicians who exercised poor judgment advised him not to make the mistakes that they had made. Presidents, governors, and Supreme Court justices, who had committed horrible deeds or stood by, and permitted others to commit such deeds in their name. Nelson Rockefeller held hostage by the ghosts of the men he murdered at Attica like Lady Wilde's "ghastly, spectral army." HST, whose generals defied his orders that no civilian areas of Japan be A-bombed. The bomb inflicted genetic damage upon generations of Japanese.

It was bad enough that President Clift reminded Americans of the Bill of Rights, with which most Americans were unfamiliar—a majority couldn't identify the three branches of government—but then he said that he was inspired by a visit from St. Nicholas. That did it. His enemies in Congress invoked the 25th Amendment to remove him from office. His vice president, Kingsley Scabb, was harassed by the End Timers, who stood, armed, outside of the vice president's mansion. They stalked his children. They issued death threats. They accused him of attending black masses in the New England woods, a charge that would have booby-hatched the rumor spreader in a former time, but now that kind of assault on one's character was right at home in what America had become. In light of the threats to him and his family, he resigned from the vice presidency. Jones urged Rapture congressmen to replace him with Jesse Hatch, the favorite of End Time evangelists. Knowing Hatch's secret, and his indebtedness to the End Times base, Jones forced Hatch to appoint him as chief-of-staff and to choose Senator Robert Sewall, a former oil lobbyist, as vice president.

Outraged, Dean Clift's thousands of followers demonstrated throughout the nation in protest but were routed by troops sent in by Hatch. People from other countries were wondering, has America gone cuckoo? Road Runner nuts? Rev. Jones became the most powerful person in America.

This was a shock to his former colleagues at Queen's College. His transformation. Clement Jones had settled into a long career of academic mimicry. Like, he had the latest theory fads down. Like, he knew the origins of words like "gaze" and "unpack." But after his father, the head of their televangelical empire, died in the arms of a hooker in a seedy New Orleans hotel, he was chosen by the church's elders to succeed him. At first, he resisted but then he got seduced by the power that came with such a position. He convinced the evangelical community that instead of giving their support to politicians who made fun of them behind their backs, calling them rubes, boobs, hicks and hayseeds, deplorable, or disgusting, one of their own should be the head of things. It was the board of directors of the church who had invited Jones to succeed his father. The only roadblock was his mother who was entitled to half of her husband's estate. Clement had a Rapture orderly cut off her oxygen at the nursing home where she lived.

One Sunday, the Elders invited Jones to deliver a sermon. He accepted the challenge. For one summer at Queens College he had taught The History of the King James Bible. He preached so well and convincingly that people were holding on to their seats and clinging to their loved ones to keep from falling into Hell. A real smart cookie, Jones soared to the leadership of the Evangelical movement shocking his former Queens College colleagues. In fact, they signed a petition, which was printed in *The New York Exegesis*, expressing their disappointment. He hadn't spoken to his father, a grifter sustained by the donations from millions of poor people who lived miserable lives. They were hoping that the Rapture would remove them from their wretched earthly existence.

But even though the majority of the evangelical community was staunchly behind the new Hatch administration, there were some who were impatient with Jones and Hatch. They were so lustful for the End Times that they were about to give the Hatch administration a deadline. To stave off such an outcome, Racub Brothers Energy got their employees, Congress and states' governors, who depended upon their donations, to overturn the 22nd Amendment.

Now that there were no term limits, the Jones administration was given more time in power. Opposition arose in the campaign of Termite Control, whose real name was Luke Lockett and who was dismissing The Rapture as a hoax.

His followers considered the Klan, whose pagan roots also lay in Northern Europe—the burning of the cross was viewed as repudiation of the invaders' religion—, too moderate. Another symbol of the Nordic resistance to Christianity was the upside-down cross. Ask your typical Klan member and he or she probably is unaware of why the cross is burned.

Rev. Jones and his people knew that Termite Control was a notorious skirt chaser. Skirt chaser? Not really. There was no chasing involved. His lovers were passive. Women that other men wouldn't be caught dead with. Rumors were that he had bribed RAHT TV not to reveal his particular fetish, but given the liberalizing trends, now, he boldly claimed it. His enemies referred to it as his Sleeping Beauty Thing. There are different versions of how Hollywood producer, Bob Krantz, became a member of the Hatch administration. One has it that Clement was on his way back to his Los Angeles hotel after a fundraiser held by End Times actors in Malibu, when he came upon a burning vehicle. Rev. Jones rushed from the black SUV, one of the vehicles in the Jones' caravan. Thinking that the driver, Bob Krantz, was still alive, he opened the door. In between Jones leaving the SUV and Krantz's death, an alien from the exoplanet Dido had assumed Krantz's body.

It was all over the Legacy media. Social media even claimed that Jones lifted the car which had Krantz pinned underneath. TV, the internet, and phone texts announced that Rev. Clement Jones had rescued Bob Krantz. The Didonian Krantz and Rev. Jones became close and Jones brought the alien, who was now installed in the body of Bob Krantz, to the White House. Jones appointed the alien Krantz as White House communications director, but soon he was made head of the National Security Council. With this position, Krantz started off with a bang, insisting that the nuclear arms race begin again, in keeping with the Didonians' plan to end the earth's menace to the universe by promoting nuclear war. He became a leader of the Hawks, advocating the placing of more nuclear weapons in space.

Jones had learned to distribute red meat to his followers with the best of them. Under the direction of Krantz, the administration concocted a plan that went by the code name Operation Two Birds. Krantz persuaded Jones that he would delight the evangelical base by ordering the bombing of New York, seat of the eastern elite—people who preached evolution, turned up their noses at Joe Six-Pack and Nancy Walmart, bought coffee at Starbucks instead of Java Joes. This would please their followers who hated New York as much as they hated San Francisco. They would blame the bombing on unnamed terrorists who had infiltrated an African country. Admiral Matthews became aware of the plot and signaled that he would expose this plan at a press conference, but before the conference was to be held, the Admiral turned up dead. The plot was exposed however in a letter found by the Admiral's maid, and, never one to take responsibility, Jones blamed the whole thing on Bob Krantz and the Admiral, the late Admiral having become the mentor to Krantz. Clement charged them with being members of "the deep state." While on the run, Krantz was visited by two emissaries from Dido to remind him of his mission. From *The Terrible Threes*:

The barbarians are about to invade our planet. It's being taken over by the yellows. We Blacks and Whites have no place to go. You were supposed to start a little nuclear action here so that these cockroaches on two feet would be removed and there'd be room for us. But you've become sidetracked over such issues as loyalty and now love. Loyalty to Reverend Jones because he saved you from a burning sports car.

"He's responsible for the death of his mother. It's bound to come up sooner or later," the Black one said. "He what?" "He hired an orderly to abuse her in a nursing home or something. Anyway, we checked him out," the White one said. "Maybe that will cure you of your addiction to earthly habits. Phony. They're all scoundrels. Not one of them without larceny in his heart. The sooner we get rid of them the better," the White one said. "Maybe you're right," Krantz said, stunned. "Now you're beginning to see it our way," the Black one said. "We'll give you another chance. Pretty soon Jones will need all of the help he can get."

Rev. Jones had appointed Rapture judges who were opposed to a woman's right to choose, sending women once again to back-alley jobs and Mexico. The Rapture judges were the majority on the Supreme Court, including Justice Nola Payne who was considered a gender traitor for voting against women's rights. Dean Clift gave fossil fuel moguls free rein. Rev. Jones's coalition continued their slow-motion soft and sometimes violent extermination of Blacks, Browns, and Reds. But what held the End Times coalition together was his promise that the Rapture was imminent. But then came a BOMBSHELL!!! Supreme Court Justice Nola Payne also had been visited by Nicholas, but seeing the reaction from his enemies to Clift's announcement, she kept the visit to herself. She shocked the nation when she sided with the remaining Clift faction on the Supreme Court by casting the deciding vote that restored Dean Clift to power.

While other members of the Hatch administration were gathering their passports for the purpose of choosing exile rather than Clift's people indicting them for corruption, afraid of losing power, Rev. Clement Jones threw a Hail Mary. He made an alliance with the Devil, who'd been hanging around since he and his Native American followers were thrown out of Europe after the triumph of Christianity according to

St. Nick shows Nola Payne Roger Taney's fate.

Puritan thinkers. In exchange for his interrupting Clift's return to D.C., the Devil would also provide him with unlimited opportunity. But on a date agreed upon, he would give up his soul to the Devil, if the Devil kept his side of the bargain.

Huge crowds stood along the route of the caravan that was to bring President Clift from the sanatorium where he had been taken by his enemies. A triumphant parade down Pennsylvania Avenue had been planned. Those who were concerned about the repression of the Civil Liberties that Clement Jones and his henchmen had erased welcomed the Clift Restoration as it was being called after the years of wiretapping, spying, and general persecution of those citizens who had not accepted the Christian faith. The Rev. and his government had almost succeeded in getting their corporate friends to put pressure on their Congresspersons to pass the Conversion Bill that would require all citizens to convert to Christianity or be deported. They always fell a few votes short, but enthusiasm for the measure was gaining. It was decided by some Christian scholars that the notion of Freedom of Religion was of pagan origin. Created by Genghis Kahn. Among the books in Thomas Jefferson's library was a biography of Genghis Kahn. The Rapture leaders were considering the removal of Jefferson's statue from the Capitol. Not because he was inspired by the pagan Genghis Khan, but because he was a race mixer.

As Clift's entourage began its drive from Virginia into D.C., those who had been driven underground a decade before came out into the open. Those thousands who had been driven to seek exile in Canada and elsewhere were considering a return. Not since the administration of JFK, the American Arthur, had such hopes stirred in the breasts of Americans. But just as that administration ended—The Terrible One—with the assassination in Dallas, because following this assassination, suicides and divorce rates increased and distrust of the government settled in when some of those who might have been involved in the assassination of JFK were assigned by LBJ to be members of the commission established to investigate the murder. This became the origin of QAnon, for whom the word Pizza meant more than pepperoni and melted cheese laying on flat bread. The hopes of Clift's followers were crushed when it was announced that Clift's entourage had disappeared on a freeway somewhere in Maryland, evidence that the Devil had kept his word.

For Nance Saturday, such metaphysics—full of devils, goblins, witches, and ghosts—were off-putting. A
man of numbers, his god was Exactitude. His position
on the autism spectrum provided him with a skill in
math that baffled experts. When he was two years
old, without hesitating, he could tell you how many
seconds were in a year. He'd mastered Trig, Calculus,
and Algebra by the time he was seven, thanks to his
uncle and his "mothers" who were living in a polyamorous situation. He studied law but returned to
math, after sitting in on a class in calculus. He became
fascinated again with the subject. Once he became
attracted to a subject, he became obsessed. He became
a master of Astrophysics, receiving invitations to join
teams the world over, but he settled on using his math
skills to protect the financially challenged from pred-
ators. Yet rumors persisted that he had chosen that
manner to exercise his math skills because he had found
an equation that predicted an event that if earthlings
knew about it, there would be panic. Something was
headed this way.

Such was his aptitude with cleaning accounting books
that the Vatican had requested him to look at theirs. He
was recommended by a friend who was a bishop before
becoming a cardinal. Then pope. He became a cardinal
because the pope demoted the Cardinal of New York
who was accused of bloated and rich living. He lived
in an eight-bedroom, 10,000-square-foot manor house
adorned with four fireplaces and a grand circular stair-
case framed by murals and a dome painted with clouds.
It was located on seven lakefront acres, with a private

The 446-page document said that Popes Benedict XVI and John Paul II had known for years about claims against McCarrick, a former archbishop of Washington, D.C., who was one of the most prominent figures in the U.S. Roman Catholic Church.

The 446-page document said that Popes Benedict XVI and John Paul II had known for years about claims against McGarrick, a former archbishop of Washington, D.C., who was one of the most prominent figures in the U.S. Roman Catholic Church.

tennis court, outdoor pool and 70-foot indoor lap pool that resembled a Venetian canal. It was given to him by a rich couple.

The then pope tried to liberalize institutional practices within the Catholic Church, but his mysterious death was called the Second Vatican Scandal. They found Chuck Berry's biography on the pope's nightstand next to his death bed, he was so eager to be current. He was an early model for two TV series, *The Young Pope* (2016) and *The Two Popes* (2019), in which ex-Pope Benedict, who covered up The Scandal, was made to look "woke." Eating pizza, doing the Tango, and handing out Beatles' records. *The Young Pope* showed a sensuous erotic pope played by Jude Law. The musical background for the show was laced with licks from Jimi Hendrix. What does he do with a pedophile bishop? Turn him over to the police? No, he sends him to Ketchikan, Alaska, where he can possibly molest Native American children. In *The New Pope*, rap music is used on the soundtrack, and sensuous dancing and nudity are included.

Nance did his best with the Vatican books, but it was an impossible situation given the billions that the Vatican had to pay out as a result of the child abuse scandals that were exposed in the 1980s. Before the Catholic child abuse scandals began to be reported in the 1980s, ensnaring hundreds of priests, bishops and even those close to the pope, Ishmael Reed had said, in 1974, during an interview, commenting on the film, *The Exorcist*, that the idea of having an exorcism conducted by a Catholic priest was ironic because the Church itself was full of the Devil.[1] As usual, Reed was accused of going too far.

Nance did succeed in persuading some of the creditors to reduce the Vatican debt. Nance could not have dreamt that he'd be invited to the Vatican again. Invited to ceremonies around the selection of a Black pope who had been Cardinal of New York and his friend. Nance was one of his drivers. Just as Blacks had been called upon to rescue Western institutions before, the creditors that Nance was able to stave off were now satisfied. Temporarily.

---

1. "The Catholic Church created the devil, and the Church is full of the devil..." Ishmael Reed, *The Bergen County Record*, Bergen County, New Jersey, April 22, 1974.

Other Characters: Elder Marse, Boy Bishop, Saint Nicholas, Black Peter, NIX, et al.

A Horatio Alger success, Elder Marse began as a lower-level employee to its CEO at the North Pole Development Corporation. He purchased the rights to Santa Claus and hired ex-soap opera star, Rex Stuart, to perform as his Santa Claus at the North Pole Development Corporation's Christmas party held at New York City's Madison Square Garden. This brought the NPDC in conflict with a con artist who had borrowed the name of Zwarte Pete, who was the real Black Peter, who in the Dutch Christmas iconography is Nicholas's assistant or sometimes his boss. The counterfeit Zwarte Pete had operated a three-part monte game in Times Square, until Boy Bishop brought him into the NIX cult. (NIX is the acronym for the terrorist group, the Nicolaites.)

Boy Bishop, who broke from his family fortune, Rakub Oil, finds Nicholas to be his favorite Saint. This is why he takes the name Boy Bishop, which is what Nicholas was called at one time. Saint Nicholas rescued women from prostitution:

> *The most fascinating story related to current-day Santa, involves Saint Nicholas coming to the aid of a poor man who could not afford the dowry for his three daughters. Without funds, the daughters were destined to remain unmarried and would likely need to turn to a life of prostitution. Upon hearing of their plight, Nicholas decided to help the first daughter when she came of age. To avoid embarrassing the family with a public display, Nicholas went to the house under the cover of night and threw a*

*purse filled with gold through a window for the family to
discover the next morning.*

Like Nicholas, Bishop rescued two prostitutes,
Barbara and Alice, from the streets, which brought the
NIX into conflict with their incompetent pimps, Joe
Baby and Big Meat. They hired a hitman named Snow
Man to take revenge on the NIX, but the NIX murdered
Snow Man and Boy Bishop revived him from the dead
with the tears of St. Nicholas. *"Tradition has it that an
evil shopkeeper in the town of Myra hated children. He
kidnapped three small boys, chopped them up with an
axe, and pickled them in a barrel. St. Nicholas, upon
hearing of this horror, prayed fervently to God. Because
of the purity of his faith, the boys were raised to life
and wholeness again and came out of the pickle barrel
singing 'Alleluia!' and giving thanks to God."* (As found
on beliefnet)

Boy Bishop brought the con man into the NIX after
striking up a friendship with the three-card monte
operator in Times Square, on the basis of a mutual
interest in Reggae culture. He left him in charge of the
NIX while Boy Bishop fulfilled an errand, to sabotage
a luxurious ocean liner docked in New York Harbor.
The NIX considered ocean liners to be floating garbage
dumps. Both Poseidon and Saint Nicholas are associated with bodies of water.

When Bishop and his crew returned, they found
the cult divided between those who supported Black
Peter, who wanted to replace Saint Nicholas with
Haile Selassie, because of their similarities, and those
who supported Boy Bishop. Black Peter was expelled.

Seeking revenge, he stole the zombie Snowman and used him to disrupt the annual Madison Square Garden event sponsored by the North Pole Development Corporation. A ventriloquist, like his slave ancestor Pompey, had the Zombie make incendiary anarchist speeches which led to a riot. The NIX were blamed, bringing more heat down on the eco-terrorist group. Offended by this assault on their reputations, the real Nick and Pete arrived from the ether. The authentic Black Peter intervened on behalf of a drug-addicted mediocre Hollywood musician; an Asian American intellectual who had a crush on an aging anti-Stalinist member of the New York Intelligentsia, "The Family"; a turkey with severe self-esteem problems, and others. The fake Black Peter was given credit for the miracles of the real one, which spooked the fake Black Peter. He got real paranoid and began to deteriorate. Nick converted members of government by showing the misdeeds of their predecessors and warned them not to make the same mistakes. By converting Clift and Supreme Court Justice Nola Payne, Nick was responsible for the crisis that led Rev. Clement Jones to sell his soul to the Devil.

Termite Control (born Luke Lockett)

The Terrible Threes ended with the introduction of Termite Control, a worshipper of Odin who challenged Clement and Hatch. The media sarcastically dismissed his followers as "The D'Roaches," a derisive term given to Termite and his party, but all of the pundits agreed that this party, which was on the ballot in twelve states, didn't have a chance. The American people weren't that stupid. This would change.

Termite Control's dietary habits were disgusting and his idea of intimacy was obscene. Termite got his name from the name General Westmoreland applied to the Vietnamese, "Termites." Fifty psychiatrists had contributed to an anthology which questioned his sanity. Others agreed that he was a disease vector and a viral pathogen.

Esther, John and Joan: They were among the White House staff that still remained during the takeover of President Dean Clift's administration by the Rev. Clement Jones. Others had quit. Too many unexplained knockings. Apparitions. Voices coming from behind closed doors and when those doors were opened, nobody was present. Sightings of the ghosts of former presidents, most frequently Abraham Lincoln. The three acted as a chorus which commented on the behavior of Jones, Krantz, and Clift.

Heinrich was the ghost of an SS soldier that stowed away on President Reagan's plane as he returned from Bitburg, Germany, where he honored the Waffen-SS, 1985. Jewish organizations observed that while he found the time to lay a wreath at a cemetery where Nazi soldiers were buried, he couldn't find a space in his schedule to visit Dachau, a concentration camp. The ghost was Clement Jones's advisor until the Devil made him get rid of him.

Joe Beowulf was lent to Clement Jones by Towers Bradhurst. A robot enforcer, he was drawn up by one of the many techs employed by Bradhurst, whose income came from violent and racist video games.

Rex Stuart: Former star of the soap opera "Sorrows and Trials." Fired from his job for an attempt to organize the TV workers.

Vixen: Worked for The North Pole Development Corporation. But finding that her hero Santa Claus was a zombie, went far right and set up a colony of White supremacists in the state of Washington.

Oxro: Leader of the exoplanet, Dido

Lodon: Oxro's assistant

Ughol: Leader of the opposition to Dido's leader, Oxro.

Gink: Ughol's aide

Introduction

Hundreds of years before American citizens began electing people to Congress who believe that Pizza is a code word used by "the deep state," for pedophilia, and that the late JFK Jr.'s death was faked and he's advising presidents while hiding from the "deep state" in Pennsylvania, the land was rife with other conspiracy theories.

Sir Walter Raleigh in his History of the World, *written in the Tower of London in the early 1600s, asserted that some centuries before, the Americans had been "brought by the Devil under his 'fearful servitude.'" .... The eminent theologian Joseph Mede declared that shortly after the advent of Christianity, Satan induced the ancestors of North America's Indians to migrate with him to America.*

From *The Pequot War*, by Alfred A. Cave

Sightings of Hobomock, the Wampanoag trickster, persisted into the twentieth century and are still remembered... although no new folklore has been created about this figure in a long time.

Part 1

Chapter 1

The Hatch administration's attitude toward global warming was that no policy was the best because with the Rapture, there would be no need to attend to earthly things. Not even the shark attack on a man who was wading through the streets of Miami stirred the government, or a malaria outbreak in New York City. On that day in December, Manhattan's temperature was 128 degrees Fahrenheit. People, especially the elderly, were advised to remain indoors. Some people wore summer clothes as they shopped for Christmas gifts.

Ice Cream was fortunate enough to have an expensive air conditioning unit in his green room. His appearance at the Haley Awards had been a real hit. He'd won five Haley's for his Hip Hop impersonations. Already there were millions of tweets, Instagrams, etc., mostly pro, some con. Cream's girl, Gladiola, would be arriving in an hour or so and they would go to the after party. He was humming as he awaited the makeup artist who would help him spring a surprise when he entered the private party being held in his honor. He slapped his latest royalty check onto the green room table. *Look at this money. The numbers look like phone numbers. But there is more loot to be had. Tonite, I enter the party in blackface. Cause a controversy. Then apologize on Instagram. My new hit will shoot to #1 as a result.* Ice Cream leaned over and snorted a line of coke that lay on the glass top of the green room dresser. Ice Cream was interrupted by his manager, 300-pound Glock Remington, head of Crosshairs Records, formerly Acme Records, headed by a character named Big Mike (See T.3s) who'd been killed in a drive-by shooting. Glock was covered with so many winking diamonds that he resembled a walking galaxy.

"Ice. Why did you summon me here?" Glock signed up Black delineators because they brought in more money than the Black creators. People with the money to buy cultural products preferred interpretation to the real McCoy. Ice Cream's music was of the kind in which a loud bass drowns out the other instrumentation. Every time Ice Cream mimicked the voice of a Black rapper, millions of Blacks cringed.

"Hey, Glock, I got a great idea. I want to get your opinion. I go to the party in blackface. There will be a backlash on social media. I apologize and we watch the ratings."

I should bust this mo'fo in the mouf! But then Glock thought of all of the luxuries that had accrued to him as a result of his authenticating Ice Cream's appropriation of Hip Hop. The autos, one for every day of the week. The clothes. The jewelry. The mansion on Long Island. A duplicate of the one in the movie, *Scarface.* All he had to do was to give Ice Cream ghetto bona fides. Calming down, he said, "That's a great idea, Ice Cream."

"And you know your role?"

"What's that Ice Cream?"

"Well, the brothers and sisters who resent that I get awards each year as the Hip Hop star of the year will ask you to explain my political incorrectness. I've written down your response."

Glock takes the paper. "Blackness is no longer merely a biological determinant."

"I'll rehearse this on the way to the party, Ice. Thanks. When are you going to the party?"

"Tell them I'll be there shortly. I'm waiting for Gladiola to arrive from London. Boy, are they going to be surprised."

"Right," Glock said after a pause. "I'll see you there." Glock was so mad that he could have given Ice Cream some instructions from the ghetto university right there.

Ice Cream, the emperor of Hip Hop, was becoming impatient. The woman he'd hired to apply his makeup was late. He snorted a few more lines. She finally arrived but instead of the makeup person the personnel office said they'd send—a pert blonde who wore her hair tied in a bun—a middle-aged Black woman showed up. She talked with a Caribbean accent.

"I'm sorry I'm late, Sir."

"Where is the regular?"

"She call in sick today. They call me."

"Well, get busy. You know what I requested."

"Yes sir." The woman, who was Hobomock, the Wampanoag trickster, who possessed the ability to change into "divers shapes" according to witnesses who lived in the 1600s, applied the black shoe polish until Cream's face was completely black. She painted his lips white. When he completed the job, Ice Cream reached for the mirror.

"Perfect." He handed her a one-hundred-dollar tip. "You can buy plenty of beef jerky and ginger beer with that."

"I sure can, Mr. Ice Cream. I sure can do that."

Chapter 2

Ice Cream had fallen asleep. He woke up. *What time is it?*
He glanced at his Rolex Oyster Perpetual 39 Automatic
Blue Dial watch ($8,000). *What the fuck?* There was a
knock at the door. He opened the door; it was his girl-
friend Gladiola. She was as thin as a straw. Because of the
hot winter weather in New York, she was dressed lightly.
Her hair was short and brunette. She'd just participated
in a London fashion show. "Where's Ice Cream?"

"Why, I'm right here." Ice Cream reached out to
embrace her.

"Get away from me. Get your dirty Black hands off
of me. Where is Ice Cream? What have you done with
him? Help! Help!" She ran from the room.

He looked into a mirror." What the fuck!" Ice Cream
needed to scrub the black off. He wanted to surprise her.
Now she'd gone to get help. The stunt had backfired.
He'd have to wash his face until the paint disappeared.
But no matter how much he scrubbed, it remained.
Not only on his face, but his arms, legs, feet and OMG
on his You Know What! Places where the paint hadn't
been applied. He kept scrubbing. Glock could explain
but Glock had left for the party.

Commish and Mayor out on the Town

Suddenly there was loud banging on the door and hostile shouts. Ice Cream climbed through a window, scrambled down a fire escape and ran down an alley. When he exited the alley to the street, he saw his girl-friend talking frantically to New York's mayor, whose nickname was "Loathsome Larry" (T.2s), and Police Commissioner Harry Brown who happened to be passing by on the way to a brothel in Chinatown.

"There he is now," she said, pointing to Ice Cream. Ice Cream approached them. He wanted to explain, but Police Commissioner Brown began shooting. Ice Cream started running away. Ice Cream got away, but finding blood on his shirt, he realized that he had been shot. Later that evening, Nance Saturday's ex-wife, Virginia Saturday, interrupted her news program with the bulletin.

"Reports of an incident at the Bill Haley Memorial Theater, scene of the annual Haley awards. A man described as Black or Hispanic has murdered Ice Cream, the Hip-Hop star, who had earlier won six Haley awards. Ice Cream's girlfriend Gladiola said that the man tried to rape her as she stumbled upon the crime scene. Mayor Loathsome Larry O'Reedy and Police Commissioner Harry Brown, who happened to be passing by the building, attempted to capture the man. Brown believes that he wounded the culprit."

Hobomock watched the scene until the police cars left. Woke, Hobomock had an agenda. He was the original resistance fighter. While Ice Cream saw black face as a marketing device, for Hobomock, it was a serious matter. It brought up memories of an early version of the Ghost Dance that broke out in 1643. Indians painted themselves "black as coal," a sign that they'd surrendered to the English. Hobomock's resistance ended when he was cursed by Keitan, a good Indian, who imprisoned Hobomock in the Sleeping Mountain, but now his promise to return if the land and waters were abused had come true. For Hobomock, blackface was a sign of capitulation. What aroused Hobomock from his sleep? Maybe it was the white whale who was found dead, its belly full of plastic. The Wampanoag had a white whale myth before Europeans arrived in America. Or the other item might have caught his attention: "An American man completed the deepest-ever solo underwater dive May 1. But when he reached the bottom of the Challenger Deep in the Mariana Trench, he found that another representative of the human world had gotten there first: plastic." (*EcoWatch*, May 14, 2019) Victor Vescovo said he found a plastic bag and candy wrappers on the seafloor, some 35,853 feet below the surface.

Not to be toyed with, Hobomock moved on to find the next individual who had been naughty or at least had a bad attitude. Unlike a benevolent Black Peter (T.2s, 3s), who lifted individuals from addiction, Hobomock of the Wampanoags, the spirit of resistance, had awakened from his long spell. His mission: To rid America of the earth defilers.

Chapter 3

Nance Saturday was relaxing in the pope's summer palace. This was a swell room. He was leaning back under a canopy of medieval design. Had kicked off his shoes and put on a white bathrobe upon which was the pope's insignia. He'd had a sauna and was contemplating paintings on the bedroom walls. Paintings worth millions of dollars. Some of the pope's aides had brought in some fruit. He was about to fall asleep, while being serenaded by a chorus of exotic birds, when an alert came across his phone. He had forgotten to turn off the B.B.C. There had been a shooting at a gathering of evangelicals in Virginia. There were multiple casualties. After a half hour, the reason for the shooting was broadcast. Those who believed that the New Jerusalem would be established in Massachusetts, Matherites, were spraying their adversaries with Ak47s. Their adversaries, from someplace like Texas, were firing back. As you might recall, Rev. Cotton Mather in his famed sermon of 1677 said, "but this was the land that they [our fathers] hoped to make so pure and holy, that Christ would take up his abode here," a prophecy that for some came true, because in 1890 Native Americans had witnessed the return of Jesus, just as Mormon prophet Joseph Smith said they would.

The opponents of the Matherites were ducking under chairs and firing back. They believed, with the prophet Zechariah, that Jesus would appear on the Mount of Olives, not as Cotton Mather hoped, in Salem. It was like the Hilton and the Marriot at war over who would host the Messiah. Yet, another faction believed that the Elect would be gathered up to a Kingdom of Heaven, a Kingdom that would have nothing to do with earth. This growing schism reflected anxiety and confusion among the End Timers. The competing sides had been engaged in a lofty discussion about Apocalyptic Millennialism—after all many of the delegates had attended Christian schools—before some of the delegates took out their weapons.

The Hatch administration, led by Rev. Clement Jones, had promised that the Rapture was imminent. He welcomed the feud between the Matherites and those who believed that Jesus would rule from Jerusalem. That meant that his party, those who believed in the lifting up to Paradise of the faithful, a minority, could thrive. Many were getting impatient and doubting that the Rapture would ever happen. Jones' evangelical supporters, his base, were wavering and a convention had been called about whether they should endorse his rival, a candidate who was a real ladies' man in a way that most considered to be bizarre. When reporters questioned him about this peculiar sexual taste, he would say that eventually Necrophilia would become mainstream, just as other pairings, once thought taboo, had won approval. On July 1, 2020, the City Council of Somerville, Massachusetts, granted polyamorous groups the rights held by spouses in marriage. Others were marrying inanimate objects.

Termite was repulsive, but he agreed with some of the Evangelists' aims. They were willing to support him because he vowed to control the reproductive functions of women and animals, the way that things were run in the Antebellum South, which was considered the Golden Age of White supremacy. Though Clement had ended the woman's right to choose, that was not enough to satisfy the more extreme faction of the Evangelicals who insisted that American society be run the way it was run in the 1600s. Therefore, some held their noses and supported Termite. Newspaper columnists had pointed to the contradiction of evangelicals supporting a worshipper of pagan idols, but the evangelicals pled that this would only be a temporary alliance.

Some were saying that Rev. Clement, whom the Rapturists counted as one of their own, needed a miracle in order to keep the Hatch administration in office. That the billionaires, the Racub family, who had turned the government into just another one of their franchises, had run out of votes to suppress and politicians to buy and even the American public, one quarter of whom believed that the sun revolves around the earth, was becoming restless. The government was at a standstill on the premise that government was unnecessary since the arrival of the savior was at hand. In the meantime, Clement made millions preaching about the Rapture.

Chapter 4

Rev. Clement Jones was away preaching to Africans, millions of whom had abandoned their indigenous religions for those of the invaders, which had caused them great harm and, in some cases, made them the victims of genocide. King Leopold 2 was a Christian. His letter about using Christianity to tame natives has become a classic and a handbook used by settlers everywhere including those residing in the United States. It worked!

Reverends, Fathers and Dear Compatriots:

The task that is given to fulfill is very delicate and requires much tact. You will go certainly to evangelize, but your evangelization must inspire above all Belgium interests. Your principal objective in our mission in the Congo is never to teach the n!ggers to know God, this they know already. They speak and submit to a Mungu, one Nzambi, one Nzakomba, and what else I don't know.

...interpret the gospel in the way it will be the best to protect your interests in that part of the world. For these things, you have to keep watch on dis-interesting our savages from the richness that is plenty [in their underground. To avoid that, they get interested in it, and make you murderous] competition and dream one day to overthrow you.

Your knowledge of the gospel will allow you to find texts ordering, and encouraging your followers to love poverty, like "Happier are the poor because they will inherit the heaven" and, "It's very difficult for the rich to enter the kingdom of God," .... Evangelize the n!ggers so that they stay forever in submission to the White colonialists, so they never revolt against the restraints they are undergoing. Recite every day – "Happy are those who are weeping because the kingdom of God is for them."

But the Raptors were becoming depressed. Even the usually compliant Plutocrat-friendly corporate press, whose relationship to the billionaires was like that between a hungry lion and a gazelle, could not defend the Rapture government. Giving every excuse possible for the voters who were keeping Clement Jones and their Rapture cronies in power. Yet, the media that supported Termite were printing editorials that the Rapture might be part of an enormous hoax. But after one newspaper, *The American Viking*, one of the last that hadn't been digitalized, was subjected to a sacking by a Rapture mob, irate that one would dispute the event predicted in the Book of Revelations, the press that had been independent had backed off. The building that housed the press was bombed and its computer system hacked. Heavily armed vigilantes loyal to Clement Jones prevented the firemen from putting out the flames.

Chapter 5

Air Force One, now called Archangel One, upon the insistence of Rev. Clement Jones, took the Rev. and his party to the far-flung corners of the world. He was too busy to deal with the two Midwestern states and the three Southern states that were threatening to secede from the Union over the fact that the promised Rapture had not arrived. Texas, however, besieged by Mexican troops, had postponed their plan for secession. They needed backup from the Federales in case Mexicans followed their new president's assertion that the Southwest and California had been stolen from Mexico through trickery and illegal invasion. Ordinarily, South Carolina would have been the first to secede, but South Carolina still needed government help to clean up what remained of a nuclear accident at Catawba that occurred after a hurricane that was mightier than all of the preceding ones that had damaged the facility.

The battle for Los Angeles was still waging. The forces of Glossolalia were doing battle with the White supremacists and their allies, the kind of Hispanics who straighten their hair and use skin lightener. They had taken over key zones in the city, including Beverly Hills.

Chapter 6

Virginia Saturday, Nance's ex-wife was reporting:

"Fans are mourning the death of Ice Cream, about whom critics say that while Elvis Presley was the King of Rock and Roll, Ice Cream was the Emperor of Hip Hop." (The newscast cut to fans laying flowers in front of the Bill Haley Theater where the murder occurred.) Virginia continued. "A woman who was to do his make-up said that she was late because she'd encountered dense traffic on the way to the Bill Haley. She said that she considered herself lucky because if she'd been on time, she might have run into the killer. We found an old interview that we did with Ice Cream that we thought his fans would appreciate." (Interviewer, Ice Cream and Glock appear on the screen.)

Interviewer: Ice Cream, critics are saying that while Elvis Presley is the King of Rock and Roll, Irving Berlin, King of Ragtime, and Paul Whiteman, King of Jazz, you are the Emperor of Hip Hop. Some of the Black critics are saying that both ideas are laughable. What do you have to say?

Before Cream could answer, Glock jumped in.

Glock: May I entertain that question. They're just in the hatin' business. None of them with their limited abilities can measure up to this artist. When he brought his demo to my office, he was so hungry that he could hardly walk. I took him to Red Lobster and bought him dinner.

Ice Cream: It's Glock who made me what I am. And now, my album, "Plastic World," has been nominated for a Grammy. Who would have guessed that someone from a sterile middle-class White family would rise in a Black world? And now our esteemed president, Jesse Hatch, has invited me to perform at the White House.

Interviewer: Many of your songs are against your middle-class upbringing. The two-car garage. The well-kept lawns. Residents calling 911 when a Black face appears in the neighborhood. Their gun fetish. The Termite Control for president bumper signs with a skull placed next to the words and the requirement that the whole family sit together at meals. Your latest album, "Plastic World" continues that theme. That song, "The Waffle Iron," is climbing the charts.

Ice Cream: That was the dream of your typical middle-class 50s family. To own a waffle iron. It was a matter of prestige.

Interviewer: It certainly is a compelling story. And now you're getting married to Gladiola, the top fashion model who has appeared on the covers of *Vogue* and *Harper's Bazaar*.

Ice Cream: For her wedding present, I'm purchasing a second mansion in the Hamptons. She'll have a mansion. And I'll have one too.

Glock: She's a wonderful person. And I know that they will be very happy.

Interviewer: Glock, the judge set your bail at one million dollars, which you were able to pay out of your pocket. The district attorney says that your explanation about your whereabouts when the murders took place doesn't add up.

Glock: Mistaken identity. I was at the club when the murders took place. I'm not into no East coast / West coast type of thing. The ho that said it was me is a liar. She been passed around among the brothers like a weak wet joint.

Interviewer: You've become the object of scorn for accepting an invitation from President Jesse Hatch to perform at the White House in light of the President using his tweeter account to say nasty things about Blacks.

Glock: I don't see nothin' wrong with talkin' to the man. Exchanging ideas.

Chapter 7

Police Commissioner Harry Brown and Mayor Loathsome Larry O'Reedy were seated in the back seat of the limousine driven by a discreet driver. A woman was on her knees servicing Brown. He was enjoying himself as he gripped her hair. His eyes were shut and he was panting. His shorts were around his ankles. The Mayor was asleep. He awoke momentarily and noticed an attractive Black woman walking down the street. He took Brown's badge and exited from the car, hurriedly. Well, not hurriedly. In fact, when he reached her, he was all out of breath and wiping his sweating face with a handkerchief. He bent over momentarily with a hairy hand on his right knee. He flashed the badge. He then pushed her against the wall and began padding her down and more. Upon returning to the car, he wiped his hand with some tissue. He was panting and sweating. "Bitch was on her period." Of course, Stop and Frisk had been voided by a brave judge named Shira A. Scheindlin, but these laws didn't apply to the Mayor of New York, or the Ton Ton NYPD.

Brown didn't pay attention to the mayor's remarks. The woman was finishing gratifying Brown. When the job was done, Brown kicked the woman out of the car. She ran down the alley, her heels clicking.

Mayor "Loathsome" Larry O'Reedy was nicknamed affectionately "Loathsome" because of his unwillingness to play by the book when handling the homies of New York. When he was a detective, before he'd pop some poor excuse for a human, he'd utter the words that made him a legend. "Give me something to write home to mother about." Of course, such a bellicose posture sometimes led to a mistake like when he killed a Black jogger whom he had mistaken for a robbery suspect. The police union backed him up and an Albany jury cleared him. After his wife died, he'd spent his time sitting before a TV, loading up on submarine sandwiches and beer. The tabloids pleaded with him to come out of retirement and save New York, where English was now a third language. They'd priced out the Blacks, but other groups were not that easily dislodged. He ran on the slogan of "FINISH THE JOB" by which he meant the ethnic cleansing that was begun by Rudy Giuliani and Donald Trump. A few thousand Blacks remained in Manhattan and Mayor Loathsome vowed to take care of those through harassment and profiling.

Both Brown and Larry O'Reedy, being widowers, enjoyed each other's company. They played poker together. Attended ball games together. Ate meatballs and spaghetti together, maybe some burgers at lunch. Two double-deckers with fries for $5, washed down with a big old container of Pepsi. They whored around together and would probably end up in the same nursing home. When asked by a reporter why he'd made his friend the exception to the order that Blacks be disappeared from Manhattan, Loathsome Larry would pound his fist on the podium and yell, "You let me decide which person is Black and which isn't. Now shut the fuck up and sit down." This was followed by some chanting from members of the Ton Ton NYPD of the slogan Mayor Loathsome had made famous when a patrolman walking the beat: "Give Me Something to Write Home to Mother About."

"So I told her pimp that he had to start sending her to my apartment," Brown said.

"What did he say?" The Mayor asked.

"He said that I was sticking the fork into the pie too often and that she had other customers. He said that he couldn't survive on freebees."

"So what did you do?"

"I pistol whipped the motherfucker and told him that if he didn't like it, he could file a complaint." They both laughed, heartily.

The Mayor asked the police commissioner, "Any news about Ice Cream's assassin?"

"Nothing new. There's a high mortality rate among Black hip-hoppers, but the murder of a White one is rare. There's something strange about this case."

"Why do you suppose he showed up at Ice Cream's dressing room at the Haley? Doesn't make sense."

"We're thinking that after Ice Cream received the award, he left the stage and headed for the green room. Now at the Haley one has to pass through an alley to another building to reach the green room. We speculate that the murderer ambushed Ice Cream in that alley, drove somewhere to dispose of the corpse and after removing the keys for the green room from Ice Cream's body returned to the green room to commit robberies. While the award winners were partying backstage, they'd left their valuables in the green room."

"But nothing was taken." Loathsome said.

"That's because Gladiola interrupted him with her screams."

Brown's watch buzzed. He answered. Another of the major Fossil Fuel billionaires had been slain. Sirens wailing, the pair were driven to an apartment located near the J.P. Morgan library. They were taking notes from the eighty-year-old Milford Chuck's spouse, who was in her late 30s. She was sobbing. She'd met Chuck at an opening that took place in a gallery she owned. One of the most powerful men in the country, the head of Chuck Oil, Milford Chuck had been murdered. To make it even more horrifying, his head was missing. The walls were covered with weird red crayon marks left by his assassins. "It became between you and the planet, you lost," signed The NIX. They said he'd been murdered for crimes against the planet. Earthocide. The house was crawling with police and a forensics team in white suits, which was scooping up evidence.

Brown leaned forward from the sofa in which he was seated. He was writing in his notebook.

"So you returned from the estate upstate and discovered the body? What time did you get home?"

"I think that it must have been 2:00 a.m."

"What were you doing up there?"

"We just bought the new house. I was there to meet with the decorator."

"How many homes do you have?"

"Twenty. Some in the United States. Others abroad."

"Must keep you busy."

"I enjoy it," she said. "As you know we have one of the more extensive art collections in the world."

The three stood up. "Mrs. Chuck, I assure you that we will do our utmost to find the killers—"

Suddenly there were loud noises coming from the ornate wrought iron stairway leading to the upper floors. Those members of the crime team that were inspecting the scene stopped their work. Finally, a fat youngster dressed in shorts and a short-sleeved shirt appeared at the landing followed by two men in white coats and pants. They were trying to grab the youngster. He yelled as they were attempting to restrain him, "The duck looked at the elephant. The duck looked at the elephant."

As they carried him back upstairs, he kept shouting, "The duck looked at the elephant, goddam it!"

"That's my husband's son by his former wife. She was forty when she gave birth to him."

"How many children did he have?"

"He had two. He hadn't seen his other son in years. He had detectives track him down. Seems he disappeared into a cult. He found his father's profession repugnant," she said.

Back in the Mayor's limousine he and his old friend Harry Brown sat, in a silence that was broken by Larry.

"The guy had a security set up, the Yin Yang one that President Hatch would envy. Still these eco nuts were able to get to him?"

"They call themselves the NIX. A terrorist group. Jones and Hatch had their Attorney General declare them a terrorist group."

"How do you suppose he was able to get it up for that broad? She looked as though she could give a fella a real workout."

"They found some Viagra in the medicine cabinet. Look, the guy had no problems with blood flow. He was still playing tennis. At his age. Here, I grabbed some." The two gulped down some capsules.

"You hungry?"

"I can use some chow. How about Italian?" Loathsome directed the driver to take them to an Italian restaurant downtown, located around Mulberry Street. In the 1960s, this area was occupied by artists who found the rents above Broadway too high. Now they had become home to Dior, Jimmy Choo, Louis Vuitton, Ralph Lauren. Priced out again, the artists had moved to New Jersey and upstate. Real estate interests were constantly stalking Bohemia. They'd civilize run down neighborhoods and home prices would soar. The Italian restaurant was one of the last in the neighborhood that was now lined with boutiques and art galleries, but traces of the old neighborhood remained here and there. Chuck's murder sent shock waves throughout the community of fossil fuel billionaires that had also taken to living in the neighborhood's old manufacturing lofts. The Racub family beefed up their security.

Chapter 8

Ice Cream awoke; he was sleeping under a pile of bloody newspapers in an alley. He'd lost blood from the gunshot wound. A Black man in tattered clothes and wearing shoes absent shoestrings was standing above him. He wasn't wearing any socks either. He had the smell of someone who hadn't changed his clothes in quite a while. His poverty was obvious. "Brother, you bleedin'. I'll call 911."

"No, don't. I can't go to the hospital," Ice Cream said, in a faint whisper.

"How you gon' stop the bleedin'?"

"I don't know, but I can't go to the hospital." He was shivering and would lose consciousness without assistance.

The man thought for a moment. "I know someone who can fix it. It'll cost you five hundred dollars and a bottle of Tennessee whiskey."

They picked up a bottle at the liquor store. The man escorted him to a rundown building. The "doctor" lived in this dingy nearly unoccupied tenement. He knocked on the door, which was covered with graffiti. Soon an unshaven white man came to the door. He was wearing a T-shirt on which one could see particles of food.

His pants were dirty. His fly was open. The two talked for a while, occasionally looking over at Ice Cream. Ice Cream's shirt was drenched with blood from the wound. They escorted him into a dirty room. There were fast food wrappings, empty coke cartons and whiskey bottles all over. The "doctor" instructed him to lie on a dirty mattress. The man who had brought him began to leave. Ice Cream thanked him.

"Fuck the thanks. Where is my tribute?" Ice Cream carried about $2000 around at all times. He gave the man a hundred-dollar bill and he was on his way.

The "doctor" injected him with something that knocked him out. The next morning, Ice Cream woke. The "doctor" was lying on the floor. Passed out. He had pissed on himself. The empty bottle of Tennessee whiskey lay next to him. Ice Cream's arm, his right arm, was gone! There were bandages where his arm once was. WHAT! WHAT! In the corner rats were eating his arm. He tried to wrest it from them, but their leader turned toward him and exposed his sharp teeth. The other rats got into an aggressive posture.

Chapter 9

There might be tens of billions of Earth-like habitable planets in the Milky Way. They're called Goldilocks planets. Not too cold, not too hot. The billionaire persons and the international criminal kleptocracy who run our planet, have their eyes on one. It was what Michio Kaku would call an A-1 planet. The inhabitants have been able to control their planetary systems, build cities on the ocean and in space, and on their moons. Use clean energy sources. Bring prosperity to all of their citizens, but now they were being watched.

The men and women of the planet Dido were not prepared for this intrusion. They were told that it would take thousands of years for their planet to be detected and by that time Earth's inhabitants would perish from their doomsday gene, leaving the planet to lower forms like protists, fungi, insects, crustaceans, spiders, centipedes, mites, sea hares, etc. But not only had they been detected with advanced instruments, all of their resources identified and filed by spectroscope, they knew Dido's business inside out. This is why Didonians had sent one of their own to infiltrate Earth's government. He had become the head of National Security in the administration of President Jesse Hatch. But this Didonian, who had assumed the body of Bob Krantz, after the TV producer was killed in an auto accident, hadn't delivered. Instead of promoting a hypersonic nuclear war in outer space between Russia, China and the U.S. that would end Earth's menace to the Milky Way, which his merciful superiors referred to as "Earthanasia," Krantz had become enamored of the planet. Sending messages to Dido's leaders that praised the different places he'd visited. Like: "Just left Las Vegas. It was a gas. Won $4,000 at the slot machine. Beautiful." Or, "Had some down time in South Beach. Sat in a cafe watching the celebs walk by. Partied at some of the clubs at night. It was good to get away from Washington." He was talking like that. The Elder Persons of Dido figured that he was wasting their time and now that the space probe had reached Dido there was little time to waste.

Of course, the Earth's government, which was about to send men to Mars, didn't have the capacity to launch an invasion now. Having discovered water there, before long 7/11s, Red Lobster, Chipotle, Taco Bell, Bank of America and Walmart would be setting up shop on Mars. Those ugly malls would proliferate the planet. But there were rumors of a private, non-governmental effort funded by billionaires and a new crop of trillionaires, who had hired their own scientists. Whose physicists had figured out short cuts. The space probe, primitive by the standards of Dido, had landed in one of the planet's lakes and was so filthy with plutonium that it had killed all of the sea animals. A similar probe had contaminated an ocean on Jupiter. It was suggested that the probe was sent by this private group, The Left Hand Path Incorporated.

The people of Dido were so down that the authorities were calling for a national week of prayer to the gods. The transportation system was shut down and the schools closed. Not a person appeared on the streets. Everybody was indoors awaiting the news.

The leader, flanked by his colleagues, was seated before TV cameras. All was quiet on this extrasolar planet, 153 light-years from Earth, in the constellation Pegasus. The leader looked worried.

"People of the Dido, the terrible news has reached us. We should not panic. As you know, up to now, we have successfully concealed ourselves from the menace of Earth's people, but now we've been exposed. Oh, their technology is very simple by our standards. Our space crafts have been monitoring their activities since this shaggy bunch slithered on to land, but now the day that we thought would never arrive has come and so we must prepare for the worst. We have survived many crises: asteroids, floods, incineration, but this may be the greatest challenge we've ever faced. You all know the consequences of an invasion from Earth. And now that their own planet is uninhabitable, our spaceships, whose form of relaxation is stalling in space and zipping away from their primitive aircraft equipment, informed us that they were sending a ship to explore ours. I assure you that their plan will fail, but there are grim days ahead. We mustn't underestimate these hyper-intense creatures. They have a great curiosity and once they set their minds on something, they can't be turned back.

We must be vigilant. And so, for now I am requesting that all Didonians gather about their loved ones and pray to the gods."

The leader's image faded from the screen.

The announcer said, "This has been a message from Oxro, President of the planet Dido."

As the leader adjourned to a room next to the studio, tears gathered. His colleagues, sitting with him, were surprised. He had participated in the 20-year war against the Ogachics, a race of evil marauders who hated difference and had invaded Dido to fashion the Didonians in their own image. He had survived infections and assassination attempts. Yet, after the broadcast, this soldier, this defender of a United Dido, rose from his chair, weakly, and had to be assisted. After resting, the leader again tried to rise, but weak in the knees, he sat back down. He was given water. His assistant Lodon was concerned.

"We've never faced this kind of crisis. Not even the quake that wiped our major trade center, Sa, was as much a catastrophe as this. All of our dreams and hopes for our planet will be lost as we prepare for this invasion." His assistants closed the door immediately.

Lodon, his assistant, had warned against panic, but it was spreading throughout Dido. Hoarding had begun. Though the government tried to keep the news of the space probe wiping out life in one of the planet's lakes, alarm was spreading. Besides, Earthlings had a habit of enslaving their enemies or those to whom they felt superior. They built beautiful cities only to destroy them. They bombed hospitals. Wedding parties. They engaged in rape. Children were their regular targets. Such practices had not been abandoned. Suppose they conquered Dido and enslaved its inhabitants? Pulverized their culture. Hemmed them in. Contained them. Turned their cities into places like Burlingame, Fremont, and Yuba City. Above ground cemeteries. Turned their planet into New Jersey. Filled their oceans with plastic. Destroyed their coral reefs and glaciers. They see everything in space as an entrepreneurial opportunity like mining asteroids for minerals.

Ughol, the leader of the rival party, had been watching the leader and taking notes. He and his aide, Gink, were angry. "This is what they get for meddling in Earth's business. They sent a spy there to promote a nuclear war, when all indications show that the planet is doomed anyway. Global warming is raising Earth's temperature so that entire parts will be covered by water. There was no use in sending an agent to infiltrate the American government. He's probably the one who showed their scientists our location. Maybe he was tortured. They torture people down there," Ugh said.

"I hear that they're going to recall the spy whose Earth name is Krantz. He wormed his way up to become an advisor to Rev. Jones, the man who runs the country, but he sends messages indicating that he has fallen in love with the Earth, which of course makes him an unlikely candidate to destroy it. They thought that by sending our spy in the form of a Jew, he'd have power. Apparently, Earthlings believe that Jews have magical powers. One landed from outer space and was worshipped," Gink said. They laughed.

"He, so the story goes, was sent by his father to cure Earthlings of their habits of dining on each other. Earthlings are the types who would look at a menu in a restaurant, and finding nothing that interests them, eat the waitress. But their spy, who took over the body of the Earthling Bob Krantz, a former Hollywood executive, whose body our spy assumed when he was killed in a sports car as his car rolled over a cliff in Malibu, hasn't delivered. Nobody is worshiping him and though he has gotten a spot next to Rev. Clement Jones, the government leader, he has failed in his assignment of fomenting a nuclear war that would end this mischievous planet's existence."

Chapter 10

Mayor Loathsome Larry O'Reedy's residence, Gracie Mansion. Loathsome and Harry Brown are being briefed by an expert on cults and esoteric movements. He is bald, thin and wearing a bowtie. He's giving the background of the Nicolaites (The NIX) who are being blamed for the beheadings of fossil fuel billionaires. The mayor wanted to know why The NIX were able to penetrate the security protecting some of the richest men in the world. The expert said that they were hiring some of the brightest hackers in the country and from abroad. He also said that there were factions among the Nicolaites. Some believe that frequent sexual intercourse is the route to salvation. But this particular sect, led by a character who calls himself Boy Bishop, are Ocean worshippers. Their icons are Saint Nicholas and Poseidon. They believe that oceans can communicate and are living beings. That killing one is like killing a human. That's why the ecology angle. Their targets are cruise ships and plastic manufacturers. They believe that life on Earth can't exist without oceans. The humans are one with the oceans. They are concerned about the disappearance of ocean life, threatened by polluters. That's why Chuck and other fossil fuel manu-facturers are their targets."

"That's the wackiest shit I ever heard," the mayor said.

Police Commissioner Harry Brown said, "I never heard of violence being associated with Saint Nicholas. Xmas is a season of peace on Earth. That's the way I was brought up. As for this Poseidon fellow. Never heard of him."

"Peace? Not so," the expert said. "Saint Nicholas punched a man named Arius, an Egyptian, at the Council of Nicaea ADA 325, because he did not believe that Jesus the son was equal to God the Father. In the 1800s, before there was Christmas as we know it now, masked young people would enter the homes of wealthy New Yorkers and demand food, gifts and drink. If not satisfied, they would trash the place."

The Mayor thanked him, stretching his arms and delivering a huge yawn.

"You need a ride back uptown to Columbia?" Commish Brown asked.

"No, I have my bicycle." Commish and the Mayor exchanged smirks. The professor put on his helmet and left the room.

"Mayor, we have to get these nuts before a panic sets in," Brown said.

"You ain't lying. But in the meantime, I can use a lap dance."

"Don't mind if I do." The two piled into the Mayor's limousine and drove to a New Jersey strip club.

Chapter 11

Ughol's residence, planet Dido.

"Do you think that the Earthlings have a genetic disposition toward causing mischief? Then one can see the destruction of the planet as an act of mercy. Why not take the planet out with a laser?" Ughol asked.

"Oxro wouldn't dare." Gink said. "He'd get into trouble with the Intersolar Council—their prohibition against interfering in the matters of sovereign solar systems. It has to look like a suicide. Like in their 1960s. It nearly happened. The Cuban Missile crisis."

"Bullshit. He's already interfering. What is trying to stir up friction between different factions of Earthlings?" said Ughol.

"Why don't the beings from Earth's sister planets put an end to Earth's nonsense? Invade Earth?" Gink asked.

"Well life on those planets is primitive. They're either too hot or too cold. It's because of Jupiter's size and its impact on the orbits of other planets in their system. But at the same time Jupiter protects Earth from comets, flinging them back into space.

"But if Earth continues on its suicidal path, the temperature of Earth will be like that of Saturn, another planet that shares its solar system. Too hot."

"When we run in the next elections. we can use it as an issue. Run on the platform that there should be a first strike against Earth. Get them before they get us. Use the laser," Gink said.

"But what about offending the Intersolar council?" Ughol asked.

"What good are they? Ours is the richest planet in the Council, yet we have to carry the load of the whole galaxy, bail them out of their unwise spending. Social programs. Foolish schemes. We need a laser shot. Blow the planet up," Gink said.

How do the Didonians look? They are attractive. They turn colors according to their 12 seasons. The two who were sent to warn the alien Krantz, however, wanted to start an alliance between the Blacks and Whites that would oppose the other colors. They were liquidated as soon as they returned to Dido. How do the people of Dido look? They don't have tentacles. They are not little men and little women. They are not machines that spew destruction. They are not out to eat the brains of Earthlings. Snatch their bodies. They don't create crop circles that baffle human scientists.

Chapter 12

During a press conference, Ughol, the leader of the opposition, sought to put the ruling party on the defensive by posing questions about the failure of Oxro to defend the planet against the Earth's menace. He read from a prepared statement:

> "Why hadn't the leader prepared the Didonians for this possibility when the Earthlings landed the Viking spacecraft on Mars? How they were planning to live on Mars, a planet that had been minding its own business for millions of years. Taking their hideous development obsession to a place that had been uninhabited.
>
> "Of course, Earth's government, which is about to send men to Mars, doesn't have the capacity to launch an invasion to Dido, but give them time. Oxro should have warned us when the Earthlings built a Supercomputer and began poking their noses into the universe's business. Like when they sent a space package to Venus loaded with 70 pounds of plutonium, not only threatening that planet, but citizens of Earth as well. Like when they detected Dido's silhouette and eventually laid eyes on the planet itself. When they were able to land a craft on a comet three hundred million miles away."

After he read the statement, Ughol, with Gink at his side, left the press room.

Oxro had underestimated the Earthlings. Their drive. Their ambition. Their overall hyperventilation. Their refusal to stay put. Their attention deficit disorder. They meant it when they said they wanted to reach the stars.

Oxro entered the room where the Elders were in frantic discussion, to show them the messages that had arrived in the wake of the leader's speech. Some of them were criticizing Oxro for putting the planet in jeopardy. It was he who said that the Earthlings would never find the planet. That Dido would evade them forever. That they would train their Hubbles to this part of the galaxy and discover only dust and Black Holes. He said that Earth would eventually disappear into the Black Hole which lies at the center of their Milky Way, or maybe the newly discovered Black Hole nearby at 1000 light years away, down the street in galactic terms. Besides, in four billion years, their sun would be extinguished. But now the Earthlings were on to them. They were not just a vague silhouette, detected only by a gravitational pull, and since Earth was no longer inhabitable, they want to carry their infection to the rest of the universe.

Oxro waved aside the criticism, the urgent requests that he give up his office. His strategy of sending a Didonian to start a war that would end human life on Earth had failed. The alien who inhabited the body of Bob Krantz was a big disappointment. He had earned the confidence of the Hatch government and as head member of the National Security Council was able to go about his business undetected. But when it came to his assignment, he had been dithering. Even enjoying himself on the doomed planet. He had to get answers. "Get Bob Krantz [He gave his Didonian name] up here. He has a lot of explaining to do."

Chapter 13

At the same time, Vice President Sewall was holding a cabinet meeting. He was filling in for Rev. Clement Jones, whose title was Chief-of-Staff but who was the most powerful man in the government of Jesse Hatch, a mere figurehead president. Hatch was nothing. People thought that it was a land deal that Clement Jones had over Hatch, but Hatch's and Clement's allies in Congress had ended the probe of that. Hatch was cleared by the majority Rapture Supreme Court. The Clift judges were in the minority, but occasionally Nola Payne, a Rapture judge would vote with them.

People were puzzled as to why Hatch had just about ceded the presidency to Jones. Most of the cabinet members, whose qualifications had been questioned by the press, were asleep. Others were comparing golf scores. Discussing the day's Dow Jones graphs. Grandchildren. The Second Amendment. Bob Krantz, the Didonian, who had been brought into the government by Jones, was defending his expensive travel—his latest caper, using an Air Force jet to visit Disneyland. He was being questioned by Sewall about his using government planes to fly to resorts in Florida and

California. Krantz was about to hand over a detailed expense account when he vanished. VANISHED! Right before their eyes. Poof! All that remained was a pile of clothes in the chair in which he had been seated. One of the cabinet members had a heart attack. The two who had been asleep woke up. Vice President Sewall dropped to his knees. The Secretary of Agriculture, who was from Idaho or someplace, rose and announced, gravely, "Gentlemen. The Rapture has begun." Were Jones and Hatch right? Cotton and Increase wrong?

Chapter 14

Virginia Saturday is on camera with two elderly people.

"I'm here with the parents of Ice Cream. Mr. and Mrs. T. Rice. Mr. T. Rice, why do you suppose your son was so critical of his upbringing and of you? This must hurt."

Mr. T. Rice: "He always seemed embarrassed that we were in his life. We never pried into his affairs or prevented him from playing that music endlessly, even though we didn't understand it. I guess we're out of date. Our tastes lean more toward The Platters and The Jersey Boys."

Virginia: "In his song, 'The Gun Cabinet,' isn't that an indictment of your membership in the NRA?"

Mr. Rice: "Look, Termite says that the Muslim terrorists are pouring across the Mexican border. We have to be ready according to Termite."

Virginia: "You and your spouse are Christians. Why are you aligning yourself with a man who is devoted to paganism?"

Mr. Rice: "This guy Termite is a little nutty but he's telling it like it is."

Mrs. Rice: "I could do without the potty language."

Mr. Rice: "Besides, I think that this Rapture thing is a hoax. These Rapture people have been hanging their reputation on this thing happening. Rev. Clement and this joker Hatch have been in office for as long as I can remember. No Rapture. Termite beating up that protestor? Hey, he was sending a message that Termites are not to be fucked with."

Mrs. Rice: "We're on nationwide television."

Mr. Rice: "Sorry."

Virginia: "Don't worry. We can edit that out."

Virginia: "He said that the neighborhood was stultifying. That he couldn't breathe. That leaving home was like leaving prison."

Mrs. Rice: "He said that? We gave him a good home. Saved money and sent him to college. Then he dropped out, but after a few years got a record out. Even though he said some harsh things about us, we were proud of him."

Virginia: "Now it's possible that he was murdered."

(*Mrs. Rice leans toward her husband. He comforts her. He gets the sniffles.*)

Mr. Rice: "And by a colored. That's the oddest part. He got along with coloreds. He took a colored girl to the prom."

Chapter 15

These were the last months of the Devil's lease, and so Jones was surprised to get a strange text from the monster reminding him. He didn't sweat how he would fare without a soul because he'd had plenty of practice. Besides from the note he received from the Devil, he realized that there might be an out. There were so many things on his plate. Now this. His evangelical caucus was complaining that he wasn't moving fast enough to eliminate Kwanzaa, Hanukkah, Saturnalia, and other holidays that were competing with Christmas. The most dangerous of them all was Saturnalia, which had only become a feature of Christmas time a few years before. It started out as a sort of seasonal gag. The workers and the bosses exchanged places during the holidays, but now workers had extended the gag beyond the holidays. It wasn't funny anymore. In a reversal, the bosses were being locked out. The workers were preventing their bosses from entering the premises of their businesses and running these businesses themselves. The bosses were in a rage. They were appealing to the business-friendly Hatch administration to do something.

Chapter 16

Rev. Clement Jones was seated in the Oval Office in the sky, a compartment in Archangel I, formerly Air Force I. He was examining some diamonds that friends high up in the Congolese government had given him after his evangelical crusade had come to an end in that country. They had demanded twenty-five percent of the gate. On the screen, his press secretary Buttermilk Doolittle was fending off questions concerning whether Rev. Jones had sold his soul to the Devil in exchange for riches and the interruption of the deposed president Dean Clift's return to the Capitol. Those rumors were circulating throughout the Capitol. In the past, such questions would have been dismissed as ridiculous. But there were people seated in Congress who believed that other Congressmen were drinking the blood of children in the basements of Pizzerias. Termite encouraged these rumors. Of course, Doolittle was correct to dismiss these rumors. Technically correct. He hadn't signed a contract with the Devil. It was more like a Letter of Agreement. His agreement with the Devil was that he would interrupt ex-President Dean Clift's triumphant return to the Capitol and that he'd become enormously

wealthy during the time that he leased his soul to the
monster. That time was nearing an end. He was wrap-
ping up his tour of Africa. Thousands had turned out
to hear him preach about The Rapture. That day when
a new world would replace the old one of sin and flesh.
Or as the poet Ichabod Wiswall (1637-1700) put it in
his "A Judicious Observation Of That Dreadful Comet,
which appeared on November 18,1680, and continued
until the 10th of February, wherein is shewed the mani-
fold Judgments that are like to attend upon most parts
of the World. The Wheat will soon be cleansed from
the Chaff."

The Chaff would be left behind. The pilot announced
that they had to maintain a holding pattern. The holding pattern continued for two hours. Finally, Jones
was angry. He phoned the cockpit and asked what had
caused the problem. The pilot told him to come out of
the flying Oval Office and enter the area where the rest
of the passengers, the press and the staff were seated.
He exited his compartment and noticed some of the
passengers kneeling. They were praying.

"Isn't it wonderful," one of the flight attendants said
to the Rev.

"What's wonderful?" The Rev. asked.

"Rev., Bob Krantz has been Raptured. They were
having a cabinet meeting and Krantz was whisked up
to the Lord. All of the cabinet members witnessed this
holy event."

The Rapture had begun? Rev. Clement Jones thought.
*You mean that this fucking Rapture shit is real? Maybe
that's why the Demon was sending him May Days? He*

had been bested? Himself condemned to eternal damnation? Victim of a metaphysical Jiu-Jitsu? Never to walk the Earth again?

"Aren't you going to kneel and lead us in prayer Rev.?" one of the members of the press asked. "The day that you have campaigned about all of these years has arrived. Why aren't you happy?" Rev. Clement stood there, his mouth still open. Stunned. He was trembling and sweating. He fell to his knees awkwardly and had to be aided by the flight attendant. He began the Lord's Prayer but when he got to the concluding lines—HE FORGOT THE LINES! which wasn't lost on the Matherites. Forgetting the lines to the Lord's Prayer was always proof that the Devil, in the 1600s Salem, had possessed one's soul. If you forgot the lines, you were either hanged or burned at the stake. His forgetting the lines went viral on social media. It drew the attention of Matherites, the Sons of New England.

The Sons of New England were meeting in the dining room of their private club. A Christmas tree dominated the scene. Outside, snow was falling. In keeping with the no frills attitude of their Puritan forebears, who condemned the Catholic Church for the opulence of their rituals, the tree bore no ornaments. The fireplace was crackling. Dressed in tuxedos, which some have called the ethnic costume of WASPS, they were quietly sipping their hot toddies. On the walls were framed pictures of all of the great sons of the society beginning with the founder, Cotton Mather. Plaques bore the names of the Mayflower passengers including Hopkins, Fuller, Howland and Cooke. There were no Kennedys.

The "No Irishmen Allowed" signs had been taken down a hundred years before, but not in this WASP hangout. These New Englanders had written many bloviating columns in the remaining prestigious print newspapers that condemned Hatch and his gang, but their writings were so pompous and full of big words that they only reached a small fraction of the American audience. Three-quarters of Americans cannot name the three branches of government, one of the reasons that they were susceptible to Termite's appeal, and why they didn't reject Clement and Rakub industries' removing Clift from office, a move that was drummed up by RHAT TV, which convinced its huge over-65 following that the Bill of Rights was a communist doctrine. The expert elite addressed members of their fellow elite in a prose that the 9-5ers couldn't have a beer with. Under death threats from Clement's followers, Scabb resigned as vice president. He was replaced by Robert Sewall, formerly vice president of Racub Industries. The consolidation was complete, the Rapture Party having swallowed up millions who belonged to fringe movements which competed with each other over who could field the wackiest propositions.

But now, the Hatch administration was faced by a populist uprising led by the rabble rouser, Termite Control. Smart-assed members of the Eastern elite had derisively dismissed this group as D'Roaches, but now nothing was funny. At his rallies, Termite had urged his followers to beat the crap out of the protestors, but now he was punching them out himself. At one rally he leapt from the stage and put some UFC moves on a protestor which ended in the protester lying unconscious from Termite's guillotine hold. While for some, Rev. Clement's lapse was just that of his forgetting the lines to the Lord's Prayer, his fumbling the words was not lost on Scabb and the Sons of New England. Their ancestors had burned people at the stake for less. Finally, Scabb rose to speak.

"Gentleman, we, the sons of Pilgrims, have stood by and watched our country ruined. We thought that Rev. Clement Jones, having kept abreast of every unreadable theory emanating from France, would have a moderate perspective about matters. He defied his Texas background to such an extent that his father, head of a multimillion-dollar television empire, stopped speaking to him, and dismissed him as a secular humanist, but then after his father died, he had a change of mind and took over the ministry. He changed, gentlemen. Since I was forced out of the vice presidency and replaced by Sewall, I've watched the slow corrosion of our values. Jesse Hatch is little more than a figurehead as Rev. Jones has persuaded Congress to entertain one crazy idea after another. The proposed expulsion from our country of all non-Christians. The proposal that the Army round up people and take them to church was postponed. But now we have an opening, gentlemen."

"Tell us Scabb," a portly cigar-smoking gentleman asked, the buttons on his white tuxedo vest about to pop. "It's reported that Rev. Jones fumbled the last lines of the Lord's Prayer, a clear sign that he is in league with Satan."

"Not so," another man offered. "George Burroughs recited the Lord's Prayer perfectly and our pious

Cotton, who watched the hanging, while mounted on horseback, said that sometimes those who are about to be hanged for practicing the Black Arts are coached and so making errors while reading the Lord's Prayer is not a test of loyalty to the Prince of Darkness. They saw a Black man whispering in Burroughs's ear. He had help during that recitation." The crowd accepted that explanation.

"Well, we'll drop the subject, but I still think it strange that a man of The Book, a minister at that, would forget the lines of the key prayer in the Bible."

George Burroughs professed his innocence and preceded to recite the Lord's Prayer. Suddenly, the 'afflicted' shouted that a 'Black man' had dictated the Lord's Prayer to him.

Witch-Hunt: The Assignment of Blame by Clifton Wilcox

The gathering discussed ways that they could take back the leadership of the country. They had a nice meal that included the required potatoes. Brandy was served after dessert. Scabb ended the meeting by reciting one of Cotton Mather's prayers. The diners bowed their heads as Scabb led them in prayer:

"It hath been deservedly esteemed, one of the great and wonderful works of God in this last age, that the Lord stirred up the spirits of so many thousands of his servants, to leave the pleasant land of England, the land of their nativity, and to transport themselves, and families, over the ocean sea, into a desert land in America, at the distance of a thousand leagues from their own country;

and this, merely on the account of pure and undefiled Religion, not knowing how they should have their daily bread, but trusting in God for that, in the way of seeking first the kingdom of God, and the righteousness thereof: And that the Lord was pleased to grant such a gracious presence of His with them, and such a blessing upon their undertakings, that within a few years a wilderness was subdued before them, and so many Colonies planted, Towns erected and Churches settled, wherein the true and living God in Christ Jesus, is worshipped and served, in a place where time out of mind, had been nothing before but Heathenism, Idolatry, and Devil-worship; and that the Lord has added so many of the blessings of Heaven and earth for the comfortable subsistence of his people in these ends of the earth."

Scabb concluded: "We must carry on the struggle begun by our ancestors. Heathenism, Idolatry and Devil-worship has infected our land. Satan has taken over our institutions. We must heed the warnings of our founding father, Rev. Cotton Mather, who is such a holy man that his only form of recreation was fasting."

When in New York the Devil stays at the Chelsea.

Chapter 17

The Devil, who was relaxing at the Chelsea Hotel, one of his favorite dens, remembered that dinner vividly. In fact, unbeknownst to members of the New England ruling class, he was disguised as a waiter on that occasion. Satan had set up residence in New England. He agreed with the Cotton Mather faction that when the Messiah returned, he would set up his headquarters in Salem, the scene of the crime and the abode of the holy Mather family, Cotton, and his father Increase. Maybe this time the Messiah wouldn't be so snooty and would submit to his temptations. He'd stopped off in New York to hang out with the old 70s gang, but most of them had died from overdoses and suicide. While some might take a fish oil pill to boost their immune system, this crowd gulped down some Speed or LSD, daily. Their unprotected sex led to AIDS. His kind of companions. Whenever he wanted to take a break from Salem, awaiting his old Arch enemy to descend, he'd visit New York, where he posed as a conceptual artist. He'd buy a number of items in a grocery store and sign his name to them. Mephistopheles. A gallery owner even gave him a show. He was on the way to Washington to fulfill the agreement with Rev. Clement. He would now control the most powerful man in the world. The Devil thought of how brilliant he was. Pope Francis agreed with him. He told the *Guardian*: "The Devil is more intelligent than mere mortals and should never be argued with," Pope Francis has warned. "Satan is not a metaphor or a nebulous concept but a real person armed with dark powers," the Pope said in forthright remarks made during a television interview. "He is evil, he's not like mist. He's not a diffuse thing, he is a person. I'm convinced that one must never converse with Satan—if you do that, you'll be lost," he told TV 2000, a Catholic channel, gesticulating with his hands to emphasize his point.

"He's more intelligent than us, and he'll turn you upside down, he'll make your head spin. He always pretends to be polite—he does it with priests, with bishops. That's how he enters your mind. But it ends badly if you don't realize what is happening in time. We should tell him to go away!" he said, reported Nick Squires in *The Telegraph*, Dec. 13, 2017.

Pope Francis was correct. The Devil is a real person. A real person armed with supernatural powers. Francis knew. As someone who collaborated with the Argentinian Junta, Francis had seen the Devil up close. And though the Devil was flattered by the pope's compliment, about his being polite, always the one to sample the wine before giving the bottle his approval, he had lost his ability to turn people upside down and to spin their heads arounds. Now, Hobomock had him on a leash figuratively. Leading him around. Had him twisting around like a hooked fish. Hobomock knew about the contract, or rather, Letter of Agreement. He made the Devil sign the agreement over to him. Adhering to the terms of the agreement with Rev. Jones, it was the Devil and his damned angels who interrupted the return of Dean Clift's entourage to Washington, after Supreme Court Justice Nola Payne had cast the deciding vote in the decision that the invocation of the 25th Amendment, which removed him from the office on the basis of an invisible disability, was invalid. But there had been an amendment to Rev. Clement Jones's Letter of Agreement with the Devil. That Jones could supplement the riches the Devil had sent his way by continuing his role as the nation's first pastor. He enjoyed the crowds. The caravan of black SUVs, aides and bodyguards that accompanied him on his tours. The pretty God-fearing women.

The Devil wanders around New England, lonely, bored and homesick for Europe. You might see him sitting at the counter of a greasy spoon, early in the morning. That's him in the Edward Hopper painting. To hide his horns, he always wears a hat. He likes his eggs over easy. Black coffee. Lots of bacon. He's a generous tipper. He only uses the power to spin people like a top and turn them upside down when he has to. But now, he can't even perform this trick. It all began one evening when he left the Chelsea Hotel, on 23rd Street, one of the Devil's dens, to have a drink. The Devil is not only polite, he's got taste. You won't find him in one of these one-star bars on Broadway where the favorite drink is a boilermaker, a glass of beer and a shot of whiskey. No, he was sitting in an elegant bar near the hotel having a cocktail when a man slid into a seat opposite him. He was very handsome. They got to talking and the man introduced himself as H. Hobomock. Said he was a professor of Native American Studies at a small college in Massachusetts, spending a weekend in New York. Said that he was down to see the World Trade Center Memorial. He invited the Devil to come to his hotel suite. While the Devil sat in a comfortable chair, H. Hobomock disappeared into the bedroom. He emerged in some silky pajamas. *Why not,* thought the Devil, who was an old switch hitter. He threw the Devil some green pajamas. The Devil went into the bathroom and put them on. Hobomock played one of Cole Porter's code songs. The Devil emerged from the bathroom. He removed his hat revealing his horns, a real turn off for some. But the man didn't even take notice. He tried to embrace Hobomock; Hobomock pushed the Devil away, telling the Devil to be patient and asked whether he wanted a drink. The Devil requested the Devil's drink. Gin and Tonic. The Devil took a sip. He noticed a strange taste. But gulped it down. He awoke the next morning. Upside down! Head spinning. Suspended from the ceiling! The Devil, who had for centuries turned others upside down, Pope Francis and even Bishops, was now upside down himself. Gone was the White man whom he met in the bar. Instead of a suit, Hobomock now wore the native costume of the Wampanoag. The Devil was furious. Hobomock had turned the Devil upside down. Tricked him like he's tricked in Black folklore. He had mixed the Devil's elixir in with his gin. A taste of his own medicine. He became an ordinary person with only the power to read minds. He was now under the control of the Hobomock and had to follow his orders.

"Shall we go to breakfast?" Hobomock asked.

The Devil was so angry that his ears emitted smoke.

Hobomack turns the Devil upside down.

Chapter 18

Social media lit up with reports of other ascensions though reporters had a hard time verifying these. Crowds were descending upon Washington as people arrived by various modes of transportation. There was pandemonium at Dulles and Reagan airports and at Amtrak's Union Station. The miracle was announced on the networks. Congress and the Supreme Court shut down as the Rapture congressmen and the Rapture Supreme Court justices went home to prepare for the ascension. Who would doubt that this day would come? Maybe Cotton Mather? Cotton thought that in the Second Coming the Messiah and his entourage would descend instead of the Rapture version during which the Wheat would ascend leaving the Chaff behind. I cite his sermon of 1677 when he prophesied: "Our Fathers did not in their coming hither propound any great matter to themselves respecting this world. But this was the land they hoped to make pure and holy, that Christ would take up his abode here on his second coming." The eminent theologian Dr. William Twiss shared this opinion, that when New Jerusalem should come down from Heaven, "America would be the seat of it." This was a pure Christian, this Mather. He was a man who would rather burn and hang teenage girls than sleep with them. Such restraint. Such class. The Devil possessed Cotton Mather's third wife Lydia, according to Mather. She sent for her niece to live with them, a voluptuous hot number with a chest like Carol Doda's. She aroused Mather. Bothered him. Why else would he vilify this temptress? Yes, psychologists might dismiss Mather's wife's actions as caused by depression, but Rev. Clement Jones, the real power in administration, knew that the Devil existed. After all, Satan owned him.

Mather the preacher who suffered an insane wife, Lydia. We know that she was insane because a number of historians, all males, had said so. How could we question the word of Mather, a man schooled in Greek, Latin, Hebrew and even the languages of savages—Iroquois? Had The End Times that its prophet Cotton Mather prophesied arrived?

Chapter 19

"We have an image of Puritans as cold, severe, hyper-strict and religious people, and while that's not entirely false, it's also not entirely true. From the very beginning, Early Americans were thinking about sex. The courts were burdened with hundreds of cases in which people broke the laws regarding sexual morality, such as premarital or extramarital sex or pregnancy out of wedlock. There was also a panic around a rise in bestiality!"[1]

Cotton Mather and his father Increase spread rumors about the Devil possessing their enemies. The Devil struck back by breaking up the relationship between Cotton and his wife, Lydia, by sending a temptress, a hussy who corrupted this holy man.

(Cotton Mather refers to his wife's niece as "a very wicked Creature... a monstrous Lyar and a very mischievous Person, and a sower of Discord, and a Monster of Ingratitude.")

---

1. Dig History Podcast: Puritan Sex: The Surprising History of Puritans and Sexual Practices, 10 Sept. 2017 https://digpodcast.org/2017/09/10/puritans-sex/

Increase Mather and his son Cotton are sitting in the courtroom. Except for about ten teenage girls, who are sitting in the front row, weeping, keening, rocking back and forth, shouting abominable epithets and spitting at the guards, White men dominate the scene. Men dressed in black are seated in the jury. The judge is a man. The guards are men. A man is on the witness stand. He points to one of the girls:

"The hussy sitting there put a hex on my cattle. They all died a few days after the argument that we had."

"He's a liar, your honor. I rejected his advances and he said he'd see to it that I would burn at the stake."

"Remove her from my sight," the judge says. The man on the witness stand smiles as the young woman is led away, screaming and scratching.

"Let's take a break, get in some smokes," Cotton Mather says to his father Increase. They rise and walk toward the entrance of the courtroom. As they pass, some of the men who are seated bow to Cotton, a complex man. He did not reject science; indeed, he had learned the inoculation with smallpox from an African captive, but Cotton also believed in an invisible world and alternative facts. Cotton and Increase were exalted members of the Puritan community. Once outside, the father and son walk to a window and stare out at the red and yellow New England fall.

"What's this trouble that you're having at home?" Increase asks.

Cotton pauses and takes a drag on some tobacco. "Lydia's niece came to live with us."

"So?"

"I've been plugging her."

"What does Lydia know?"

"She has some suspicions. She went to one of the Elders and asked that he pray with her. She told him of her suspicions."

"Yeah. So what happened?"

"He told her that Lydia's niece was possessed by demons. I'm one of his church's biggest contributors."

"That always works."

"Shit. If it were not for the excuse of Satanic possession, nobody would get laid around here. But that only worked for a while."

"So when did you start up with the niece?"

"The very first night she came to live with us. We were having our usual godly meal and my hands went under the table and headed right for her wet spot."

"Even under the excessive layers of apparel that our women wear? How did you manage?"

"I've figured out some short cuts."

"You must show me. And how do you manage to screw this slut with all those people living in that house?"

"She milks the cows every morning, while the others are doing their chores. While she's milking the cows, I'm out there milking her. I tell Lydia that I'm going to take a walk. Work on my Sunday sermon. She was moaning so one day that one of my daughters entered the barn. To see what was going on. Before I hid, I told Lydia's niece what to say."

"What was that?"

"I told her to tell her mother that it was one of the cows."

"Did it work?"

"Temporarily, Lydia went to her relatives in Sea Castle. She took the children with her. I told her that if she hung around, she might get smallpox, leaving me and her niece the run of the place."

"So what's it like?"

"How do they say, Holy Cow!" Increase bursts out laughing.

An Indian approaches Cotton and asks if he can speak to Cotton alone. They go to a corner and begin a busy conversation. Increase sees Cotton place a piece of paper that the Indian has given him into his pocket.

"What was that all about?"

"That was John Sassamon the Ponkapoag. He gave me a list of all the savages whom we have to keep an eye on. Especially the chief they call King Philip, the nickname they give to Sachem Metacomet."

Cotton reads to Increase from the note: "Says here that Philip is spending a lot of time drinking and dancing. Sassamon is sort of like a talebearer between the heathens and us."

"We need more Indians like him. A lot of them are surly, haughty, and insolent," Increase says.

"He's the preeminent spokesperson for his people. Writes in English and teaches his people the Bible. In fact, he's more devoted to the Good Book than some of our people. They call him the praying Indian. Says his highest ambition is to enter the Englishman's heaven. He cooked us Thanksgiving dinner. Guess what we gave him as a gift."

"What?"

"Blankets."

They laugh so that they howl.

"So are you still fucking that evil temptress?"

"No, one night, they woke me. The wife started scolding me. Said that her niece told her about us. She was shouting so the lights in the neighborhood from the kerosene lamps came on. I told my wife that the girl was a monstrous liar and a deceiver."

"What did your wife do?"

"She sent the wench away."

They reenter the courtroom. A farmer is pointing to a teenage girl who is standing and hissing at him. She is being restrained.

"And she said that for whipping her, a black cat would visit me at midnight."

The judge leans over and asks, "And what happened?"

"A black cat did come. Leaped over to where I was lying in bed and nearly choked me to death."

The judge banged his gavel and the girl is taken from the courthouse screaming and yelling.

Chapter 20

The Pilgrims said that when Christianity triumphed in Europe that the Devil fled to America. They got that wrong. They brought the Devil to America! The Devil knew that his home was in Europe. Hobomock was the head New England trickster before the Puritans brought the Devil with them. Hobomock saw the Devil as an intruder. But now, having tricked the Devil into drinking the Elixir, Hobomock had his number. Would Jones lose power?

In fact, he had reached such heights that his role as chief of staff in the Hatch administration was beginning to resemble a step down. He regarded it as a public service. The Devil didn't mind. He had signed up a number of leading American evangelists without insisting that they end their service to the Lord. Besides, he was aware of the power of the Lord's message. Sometimes using a disguise, he would attend these Black churches. He would find his feet starting to tap, his knees shivering, and once he got up and did a holiness dance that was so electric that the other parishioners made a circle around the Devil and started clapping their hands in time. He was jumping around and shuffling his feet like Sam Waymon in "Ganja and Hess." He stopped attending these churches. If he were to go over to the other side, there'd be no symmetry in the world. But even though the majority of the evangelical community was staunchly behind the Hatch administration, there were some who were impatient with Jones and Hatch. They were so lustful for the End Times that they were about to give the Hatch administration a deadline.

Since there were no term limits, the Jones administration was granted more time in power, given that the rightful president, Dean Clift, and his entourage had vanished. Moreover, Termite Control, his opposition leader, was dismissing The Rapture as a hoax. Those who attended his rallies brought their Norse horns, and horned helmets.

Chapter 21

Mobs stood before the White House. They brought their sick, they even brought personal items to be blessed: bread, hair combs, toothpaste, shoes, crutches, wheelchairs, walkers. They brought their children. They brought their pets. The security, not expecting such a rush, was outnumbered and so the mob rushed the gates. Troops had to be called to protect the White House. They were using pepper spray and mace to repel the crowds.

Across town, President Hatch was lying in bed with one of Madame Artemis's girls, named Holly. She was asleep. He was having a sip of wine, which was on a stand next to the bed. He got the call. Hung up.

"Who was that?" Holly asked, slowly waking up.

"Some foreign troll farm pretending to be calling from the White House. Says the Rapture has begun." They both laughed. But then there was a knock at the door. A Secret Service man. "Mr. President." He smirked as he said that because everybody knew that he was president in name only. "Please put your clothes on. Rev. Clement Jones needs you to call a press conference."

"Why? What's up?"

"The Rapture has begun."

"You're joking."

"Joking? The Rapture has been prophesied in the Good Book. Mr. President, you've been promising Rapture for a number of terms. Do you doubt this? Bob Krantz vanished before a cabinet meeting. All of the members of the cabinet witnessed his ascension to the New Jerusalem."

"Yes, of course. I haven't forgotten."

"Then let's go." The Secret Service man grabbed his elbow, and rudely shoved Hatch from the room. Hatch had momentarily forgotten that Rev. Clement Jones had staffed the White House and the Secret Service with Rapture zealots. Jones had returned to the Oval Office, with crowds cheering him *en route*. The Rapture had arrived. He was a hero. Now, President Jesse Hatch would join him. Hatch was in shock. He was shaking. As the helicopter approached the White House roof for landing, President Jesse Hatch could see crowds below hungry for a miracle. Eager to be vacuumed up like Krantz. All of the blocks leading to the White House were filled with people. They'd placed flowers that were a mountain high at its gates. Police helicopters were circling above. There was the smell of tear gas. Policemen mounted on horseback were driving some of the crowds away. Ambulances were stationed at strategic corners. Bob Krantz's photo had gone viral. Retweeted. Tik Toked. On Instagram. Facebook. People were kneeling and staring at his picture as it was being rolled on huge television screens at Times Square. Both Clement and Hatch witnessed the goings on in disbelief. The Rapture was real? How could that be? This was nothing but some crazy superstition. Yes, they'd used the idea of the Rapture to win elections, but that was about politics. Hell, millions of Americans will believe anything. All you have to do is repeat a lie. And why would Krantz be the one selected to enter Paradise? He thought that Jews had to be converted and as far as he knew, Krantz didn't identify with any religion. He shrugged off the criticism from other Jews that he was collaborating with an anti-Semitic administration. They were referring to him as a Mnuchin, the name that became synonymous with a Jew who collaborated with an anti-Semitic administration. As he was helped onto the roof, his knees went weak. Jesse Hatch entered the Oval Office. Clement and some of the cabinet members were watching CNN. Seeing Hatch, annoyed, the Rev. said, "I told you to knock before you entered the Oval Office."

"Sorry Rev., came over as soon as I could. What's all of this talk about the Rapture?"

"I can't figure it out. I dozed off on the Archangel and when I awoke the miracle had occurred. Krantz had been called home. It happened at a cabinet meeting. Everybody present witnessed it."

"Nonsense. You know the Rapture thing is junk. We just use it to get our people elected. What's all of that singing, I hear?" Hatch asked.

"People are across the street singing hymns. Some of the Termite people are there. They are calling the whole Krantz thing a hoax. They're singing songs to Odin. They were closing in on our ticket, but now that the Rapture has happened, an event at which they scoffed, they're in disarray. The Attorney General has made arrests. Termite Control is on the lam. They were thirty points behind according to the polls? That was the situation before I departed for Africa."

"While you were on your tour of Africa, Termite held a gun to one of the Rapture protesters' heads. The crowd went wild. His poll numbers climbed by 20 percent. But because of the Krantz thing, their campaign will collapse."

"This Rapture thing can work for us, but are you sure that it's on the up and up?" Jones asked.

"All of the cabinet members witnessed it." Hatch and Jones continued to watch the chaos that had erupted as a result of Krantz's ascension.

Chapter 22

A fleet of limousines awaited Elder Marse, the toy tycoon, as he emerged from the gates of a federal prison. Some of the federal judges who were not Rapture had convicted him of endangering children by placing toxic toys on the market. Like some of those who knew of the danger of their products but failed to inform the public or even lied—cigarette executives, fossil fuel manufacturers like Exxon Mobil, who knew that their products would lead to global warming and drug moguls, who continued to push OxyContin knowing full well that they were addictive without informing the public—Elder Marse had placed toys on the market that had led to deaths and injuries of thousands of children. How could someone be so low as to push products knowing that they would injure or cause the deaths of children? A report issued on March 28, 2017 sized up the problem: "Approximately a quarter of a million visits are made to US emergency rooms each year due to toy-related injuries… many thousands of injuries each year are in fact due to defects in the manufacture or design of toys, and, under product liability law, designers and sellers of such toys can be strictly liable for any injuries caused." It was discovered that Elder Marse's North Pole Development Corporation knew about the hazards presented by their toys, but got their buddies in the Hatch administration to okay their products. A friendly Federal judge, a golfing partner, sentenced him to a year. Eight months off for good behavior.

All of the executives arranged for him to party in his country manor in upstate New York. It was one of these Tudor numbers. It even came equipped with a moat. The guards whom he had bribed to bring in cocaine, girls, and his favorite truffles, steaks and cheesecake and wines from the cellar on his estate hated to see him go. He livened up the place. He had also been convicted of bribery of foreign officials, extortion, price rigging and violating labor laws. His workers in the Third World had to work 12 hours a day for one dollar a day and lived 16 per room in barracks that were located on the grounds of his property. He called his Santa Claus to proceed with Xmas. He had bought the rights to use Santa Claus exclusively, though many could be seen wearing Santa Claus caps and when those crowds appeared, they were assaulted, but then the Spirit of Saint Nicholas had appeared to convert some of the meanest cusses in Washington. But now his friend Jesse Hatch told him that Rev. Jones' scientists had broken down Nicholas's particles, the particles that allowed him to switch back and forth from visibility to invisibility and placed him in the same place where they'd previously hidden Dean Clift. Where he had been held before he and his entourage left for their triumphant return to Washington. And so, the confusion about who was Santa was cleared up. He ordered the North Pole Development Corporation to prepare for the annual Christmas pageant in Madison Square Garden, but he was told that Saturnalia had spread. That his businesses were being run by the workers and they'd locked out the managers. They were creating safe toys.

Chapter 23

The mood of gloom had been lifted from the temperament of all liberty-loving people upon the report that Rev. Jones' administration would have to leave office. But as Clift's entourage began its drive into D.C. from the Virginia sanatorium where Clift had been placed by his enemies after their invocation of the 25th Amendment—impeachment having been found to only boost the poll numbers of a president—those who had been driven underground came out into the open. Those thousands who had been exiled in Canada and elsewhere were considering a return. Not since the administration of JFK, called the American Arthur by his followers, had such hopes stirred in the breasts of Americans. But just as that administration ended with the assassination in Dallas, The Terrible One, their hopes were crushed when it was announced that Clift's entourage that was supposed to be greeted with cheers had disappeared on a freeway somewhere in Maryland. It was thought that only Clift could reverse the trend in Europe, where Far Right parties were returning Europe to its pagan roots. Europe was sounding the pagan kettle drums again and the Germans were threatening to march out of the forest as neo-Nazis were gaining power. Odin and Siegfried were becoming more popular than the founder of the West, Jesus Christ. But with this Rapture thing, their movement would suffer a setback. Of course, Termite Control's Norse mythology, like Christianity, had its idea of a final reckoning as well. Ragnarök, a series of future events, consisting of a great battle foretold to ultimately result in the death of a number of major figures (including the gods Odin, Thor, Týr, Freyr, Heimdall, and Loki), the occurrence of various natural disasters, and the subsequent submersion of the world in water. Was the new pope, a Black man, the West's last hope? Nostradamus predicted that a Black pope would appear before the Apocalypse.

Chapter 24

As in the case of other failing Western institutions, a Black person was chosen to rescue the Vatican, like Bobby McFerrin rescued a symphony orchestra, and Barack Obama postponed the fall of the American Empire. And Black mayors who were elected to run cities abandoned by industries and money.

In Europe and the United States, people were leaving the Catholic Church by the thousands, but church attendance was soaring in Africa and South America. These examples weren't lost on some of the more enlightened Cardinals of the Catholic Church. Now, the College of Cardinals, those left after the arrests, had selected a Black Cardinal from New York to ascend to the papacy. He was opposed to Cardinal Adrien from Spain, a power leader of the Right.

Miltiades II owned two miracles that occurred during the time he was a Cardinal. When visiting a Catholic hospital in New York, he was taken on a tour of the morgue. As he passed a corpse, lying on a table, the corpse rose and kissed his hand. The man who had been declared dead got dressed and went home. The only problem was that the man who had been revived began to stalk the Cardinal. Not exactly stalked, but showed up wherever the Cardinal appeared. Rushing toward him to kiss his hand.

Next, he walked into the midst of gunfire between two rival gangs. Bullets were flying at him from all directions, but none struck him. So impressed were they with his example, the gang members dropped their weapons and joined the Catholic Church.

Pope Miltiades II had taken the name Miltiades after the Black African Pope who converted Constantine (though Constantine continued to worship Apollo on the side, just in case).

Miltiades II's predecessor had taken ill and died. Rumors held that he was engaged in a spiritual house cleaning, but was deemed too progressive for far-right Spanish bishops led by Cardinal Adrien, successors to those who gave the world the Inquisition. Was he poisoned? One pope had already been arrested when found outside of Vatican City, hauled off to The Hague for covering up crimes against children.

The Black Pope, who had taken the place of the New York Cardinal, who had been forced out, insisted that the Vatican be exorcised before he took up residence there. And so he was living in the summer palace, until the exorcism had been completed. Vatican City had been sealed off. Its buildings could be seen expanding and contracting, as the Devil was resisting the work of a battalion of priests who had been assigned the task.

Apostolic Palace of Castel Gandolfo, the pope's summer residence, is quite a layout. A 17th-century building designed by Carlo Maderno for Pope Urban VIII. The

Pope had a view of the coastline of Lake Albano, where the residents go canoeing and kayaking. The location had a Mediterranean climate. Mild winters and springs. The lake was packed with carp, perch, trout, pike, and tench.

But in Vatican City, the situation was far from pleasant. Some of the priests could be seen being carried out on stretchers after losing a battle with the demons. The evil howls and groans from Vatican City could be heard throughout the city. This resulted in a long line of refugees. This was cutting heavily into the tourist business. No longer could cab drivers and the limousine services that provided rides from the airport overcharge unsuspecting visitors. Business was slow. Romans were surly, like the clerks at the front desk of the Best Western in Vatican City. A hotel where you were likely to find your laundry missing. The waiters in the restaurant, however, were courteous. Nance gave the place three stars.

The exorcism had been going on for a month, because the Devil's copycats and duplicates had been residents of the Vatican since its beginning. They were there when popes waged a 200-year war against independent women known as witches. They were there from the Church's beginning, led by Peter, who refused to recognize Jesus as he was arrested by the Romans and had a falling out with Paul, yet it's Judas who gets all of the bad press. They were there listening to the prayers of Pious XII when he was praying for a Nazi victory in Russia. When Abraham in Decameron goes to the Vatican, what does he find?

"...he found all, from the highest to the lowest, most shamefully given to the sin of lust, and that not only in the way of nature, but after the sodomitical fashion, without any restraint of remorse or shamefastness, insomuch that the interest of courtesans and catamites was of no small avail there in obtaining any considerable thing. Moreover, he manifestly perceived them to be universally gluttons, wine bibbers, drunkards and slaves to their bellies, brute-beast fashion, more than to aught else after lust."

They were there when Jean-Paul and Benedict warned priests throughout the world not to talk about children who had been molested by priests. Miltiades II had promised to continue the reforms of his predecessor. A married priesthood. Women priests and cardinals. St. Paul in his letter to St. Timothy endorsed a married priesthood. In the early Church, clerical celibacy was not mandated. St. Paul in his first letter to St. Timothy wrote, "A bishop must be irreproachable, married only once, of even temper, self-controlled, modest, and hospitable" (3:2) and "Deacons may be married but once and must be good managers of their children and their households" (3:12). "However, one should not erroneously construe this teaching to mean that a bishop, priest, or deacon had to be married; St. Paul admitted that he himself was not married (1 Cor 7:8)." He wanted to abandon the Canon 352-Council of Laodicea, which decreed that women are not to be ordained.

He and Nance Saturday, part time troubleshooter and airport limo driver, were dining in a room of the Summer Palace. The pope had hired investigators to inspect the Church's assets, both visible and hidden. The money amounted to hundreds of billions. He was deciding about how to liquidate this holy money and distribute it to the poor.

"You'd better be careful, Your Excellency. Your predecessor might have been poisoned," Nance said. He had come to know the pope when he was the Cardinal of New York. Had often driven him around the city, before his business was replaced by Uber. The pope had invited him to his installation ceremonies. When he heard that Nance was lodged at Vatican City's Best Western, he sent a car for Nance, which brought him to the Summer Palace, where he was provided with a room.

"I know that he was poisoned," the pope said. "I was there. At his bedside. He had difficulty breathing, and his organs began to shut down."

"He was a hated man. After he had ended the Vatican bank's practice of laundering drug money, he was a marked man," Nance said.

After breakfast, Miltiades II walked slowly to a window and lit up. He wrung the match until the light was out. Remembering his only vice, Nance had brought him a couple of cartons of Lucky Strikes. Miltiades II admired one of his predecessors, but his legacy would be permanently scarred, because he awarded sainthood to Junipero Serra, a Spanish priest who was partially responsible for the extermination of the California Indians.

The two had spent the day walking around the gardens of apricot, peach, and olive trees, and greenhouses of ornamental flowers. They inspected the organic farm filled with cows, free-range hens, cockerels, and bees.

Nance brought the pope up to date about what was happening back home. The new wave of Black artists whose works were on display at museums. Who was performing in Jazz clubs. The pope had one of the most extensive Jazz collections. Nance told him about some of the new restaurants that had opened. As they were walking back into the Palace, the pope paused.

"Who are these Nicolaites?"

"Oh, they're some kind of eco-terrorists. They've been blamed for the murders of a couple of coal and oil tycoons. Mayor Loathsome Larry O'Reedy and Police Commissioner Brown have promised early arrests."

"Those two are characters alright. Is it true that their leader, Boy Bishop, leaves a note at the scene of the crimes?"

"'It came between you and the planet, you lost?'" Nance said.

"The name Boy Bishop. Why does their leader call himself that?"

"They're followers of Saint Nicholas, and that's the name he was called at one time."

"Yes. Amazing. This is an example of a good cause being corrupted by extremists. They should organize voters who feel as they do."

"They tried that, Pope. The electoral system has been corrupted by big money. The fossil fuel industry owns Congress and some members of the Supreme Court, apparently. They own the media."

"Nance, you're not telling me that you side with those who believe that murder is the solution to changing public policy? Why are you siding with extremists?"

"Jesus Christ was an extremist. At least that's how the Romans saw him. He was murdered because of his extremist ideas."

"Nance, you stick to your detective business. I'll do the theology." A nun refilled their coffee cups.

"This summer palace is really beautiful. The public doesn't know about it." Nance said, changing the subject.

"The White popes built this place so that they could worship the Black Madonna in secret. They come here to pray for lottery numbers and for her to guide them to young men who wear tight fitting Calvin Klein jeans." They laughed.

Chapter 25

That night, Nance dreamed that he was in an arachnoid mode. He was concerned about the pope's safety. The conspirators didn't see him because he was curled up in the corner of the ceiling, and heard one of the servants and a high Vatican official discuss how to get rid of the second Black pope. The Spanish Cardinal Adrien seemed to have been doing all of the talking.

A mosquito almost gave his position. He had to entangle the poor creature and watch it struggle until it died. But he hung there long enough to learn that there was already a conspiracy against the Black pope. One of the conspirators referred to Miltiades II as an ape. Another was upset because the pope had eliminated the anti-Semitic Latin mass, which had been revived by a previous pope, who had been a member of the Hitler youth. Cardinal Adrian did all of the talking. He didn't like the young Black pope's CD collection. Jazz. Didn't like the clothes he wore which were created by Black fashion designers. He'd made the cover of Vogue.

He woke up from the nightmare. His night clothes were wringing wet. The next morning, busboys carried his bags. They were followed by Nance and

Cardinal Maladori. Maladori was tall and thin like John Carradine. The same triangular face like the old cartoon character Submarine man. He seemed to always have a sparkling glint in his eye. "The pope has rescued us. Holiday Inn, Hilton and even Hotel Six were looking to turn the city into a resort. Disney was about to win the bid. But copycat devils occupying the Vatican dissuaded them. It took this pope to exhibit the horrors that awaited such investors. The overwhelming smell that has led to thousands of people leaving Rome. It's inexplicable. No one knows the source. Can you imagine a pope standing by, as this ancient city was being auctioned off as someone dressed as Mickey Mouse looks on with his huge eyes?" Nance thought of what happened to New York after it was handed over to developers. Where there was once a deliciously sinful Times Square, there now stood an antiseptic district that resembled a creationist theme park. How did the brilliant Samuel R. Delany put it? He complained about the loss of a libertine Times Square.

"Don't worry, we've made arrangements with Alitalia," Maladori said. Nance thought. *They have a reputation for losing luggage. They lost Nancy Hanrahan's luggage. It was only through the intervention of Ruben Blades that the Hanrahans were able to retrieve Nancy's luggage from the woman to whom it had been delivered by mistake.*

Cardinal Maladori said, "They'll expedite your passage to the plane. All you have to do is show some I.D." A shiny black BMW showed up.

"May I give you some more advice," Nance said.

"Yes."

"You're really going to have to get your priests to stop putting their hands on children. You've lost a lot of money and land as a result. That 600-million-dollar settlement the Los Angeles Archdiocese had to pay out to victims of priests who couldn't control their warped desires. But you were right in convincing the cardinals to elect a pope from Africa, Miltiades II. He might provide a synthesis between two great religions."

"I don't follow Nance. There is only one religion and one God."

"Skip it," Nance said. He'd given up on trying to educate Westerners, so comfortable in their Eurocentric huts.

"Something to think about," the Cardinal thought. "I must make note of this."

"And you might also consider substituting the cross with the original symbol of Christianity, the fish. People find a symbol that represents someone in the state of an overdrawn execution, a turn off."

"Won't you help us in our effort against the sons of Islam?"

"Look Maladori, you wouldn't have your theology were it not for Muslims and pagans. Al-Fārāb, 872–950 AD, and Aristotle. Where do you think Thomas Aquinas got his ideas from, the tooth fairy? And you wouldn't have this grand place had not Miltiades I converted Constantine."

"Now Nance," Maladori said in the kind of patronizing voice that you get from some Whites who believe that all of the planet's wonders were created by them, a kind of ethnocentrism. They refused to give credit to the Arabs for Algebra and Trigonometry. "Nance, His Excellency has a request." Momentarily an aide appeared with a slender object wrapped in black leather. "He wants you to make a delivery. The address is here." The aide loaded the package in the trunk of the car that would take him to the Rome airport.

"One more thing, Nance."

"What is it Cardinal?"

"We asked you to come over and look at our books some years back? What did you find?"

"That's between me and the late pope and he's dead. Anyway, I helped stave off the creditors for a while, but now that you have a Black pope, the coffers will fill up. His election is seen as a nod to multiculturalism. But you got to get rid of the Devil's copycats who have taken over the Vatican. Then he can leave this residence, the Summer Palace."

And just as the Cardinal predicted, Nance was escorted to his plane instead of having to go through security. He was booked in first class and catered to by beautiful airline attendants who pampered him until he arrived at JFK. Was this a new Alitalia?

Chapter 26

When Nance returned to JFK from Rome, he saw crowds of people gathered in front of the airport's newsstands. He purchased a newspaper. When he entered the baggage claim area, he found a tall man in chauffeur's outfit, black boots, gray gloves, the works. He was bearing a sign that carried his name.

"Who sent you?" Nance asked.

"An admirer," the young White man said. They went to the carousel, where the luggage from Rome would come down a chute. Everybody who was a passenger on Alitalia got theirs. His was missing. He filled out a form. They promised to deliver within 24 hours.

When they were near his home, he noticed lines of people outside of his apartment building. He rolled down the window and asked what was going on. A young man who didn't recognize him said, "These people are trying to get in to see Nance Saturday, the man of numbers. They've been swindled by subprime loans."

"I've been away in Rome for nearly a month. I need a little rest before I can tackle these obligations."

The young White man said, "Our anonymous donor felt that you'd be bushed. She's arranged for you to stay at a luxury hotel downtown."

"I don't follow?"

"She wants to hire you as a troubleshooter."

Nance thought about it. His trip to Rome had run up his American Express debt. The chauffeur assured Nance that the five star hotel had his reservation, but to make sure accompanied Nance to the reception desk and verified it. Told him that he'd pick him up the next day and left. He was given keys to a suite. He told the Concierge that his luggage might be arriving from the airport and to bring it into his room when it arrived. He got into a jumpsuit, which he had placed in a carryon in case his luggage got lost. He also had some dental supplies. Fixodent. Brushes. Toothpaste. He had an extra pair of pajamas. As he was brushing his teeth, there was a ring at the door. Maybe his luggage? No. One of the hotel people rolled into the room a table upon which was a tray with some snacks, a pot of coffee and a newspaper. He was startled to read the headlines. It featured a picture of Bob Krantz, the former Hollywood producer. Something about his ascension. A state of Emergency had been declared in Washington because of so many people descending upon the city as a result of the miracle. Nance dismissed this news as just another outburst of American mass hysteria. There were candle-light gatherings in the parks. There was more Rapture news. Nance was back home. A country where truth and fiction were always trading places. He fell into bed and before long was asleep.

Chapter 27

The next day, the chauffeur who had deposited him at the five star hotel picked him up and took him to a townhouse located near the Frick Museum. It was a French neoclassical townhouse.

"I thought you were taking me home, why are you stopping here."

"She has a job for you."

"Who is she?"

"You'll see." Her aide escorted him into a large reception room whose walls were covered with paintings by the masters. He recognized some of them. Many of them showed Pan in a forest setting surrounded by some plump rosy colored nudes. Soon the widow entered the room. She was all there. Before he married her, Chuck had given her expensive gifts. A gallery owner, she had been his consultant. Guiding him as he purchased art. He'd divorced his wife of thirty years. She had two children from a previous marriage. One was mentally challenged. The other had endless quarrels about his father's profession. They had heated arguments which led to the stepson's estrangement. He was provided with a handsomely endowed trust in

It was the House of Chuck.

exchange for his staying away. After her death, Chuck became the guardian of the other son.

She showed him to a seat on what looked like something from an older French empire period. "I called you because you come highly recommended. As you know, my husband, the chairman of Chuck Oil, was murdered. They've yet to find his head."

"Yes. I read."

"The mayor and the police commissioner have entered the case." He glanced at the painting above her head. "Bacchanal before a Statue of Pan," by Nicolas Poussin. Showed some men and women partying before a statue of Pan looking down.

"But I want you to look into it as well. Find out who committed this awful crime. I'll cover all of your expenses."

"What's wrong with the mayor and Police Commissioner, Brown?" Nance asked.

"I've had them followed and they, well let's put it this way, they're not focused on the case."

Damn, Nance thought. *Rich people are so powerful that they can spy on the police commissioner and the mayor.*

On her phone, she even showed him a video of their activities over a twenty-four-hour period. She'd even had an App made. Nance examined the pictures. There was a video of Mayor Loathsome who had climbed on the stage of a stripper's joint and was gyrating his hip against one of the dancers. Brown and the mayor snorting coke in the back of the official limousine. Nance thought about it. He could use the case. "You can pay me half now and half when I find the culprits." When he saw the amount on the check, he nearly jumped up to say *Gaaaaaa leeeee.* But he maintained his cool. She stood up and escorted him to the door. They shook hands.

Chapter 28

Rev. Clement Jones was pacing up and down. Stroking his chin. Looking out of the window at the crowds that had amassed in front of the White House, when an evil smell swept the room. Like rotten eggs. He turned from the window and saw that the Devil had entered the room. He was accompanied by Hobomock, who had turned the tables on the Devil.

"Gentlemen, what can I do for you?"

He seems awfully confident for a man whose soul was about to be acquired, leaving him vacant and a walking dead, the Devil thought.

"Clement, this is Hobomock. He's the spirit who resisted the Pilgrim invasion. He has been asleep in Sleeping Mountain for centuries but the bad land management of Americans..."

"Get to the point, Devil, I'm a busy man."

"Enough of the talk, tell him the deal," Hobomock growled.

"I drank the Devil's Elixir, which he mixed in with my gin and tonic. True to the legend, I was rendered ordinary. You'll notice that I just didn't appear like in the old days. We flew down on the commuter. Hobomock now owns your soul. He's willing to compromise if you yield to his demands."

"Really. And what might those demands be?"

Hobomock read from a sheet: "Your first assignment will be to clean up the mess that you and the rest of invaders have made of this country. After you do that, you can go back to Europe. And so that you won't feel lonely, the Africans can go back to Africa. The Asians can return to Asia. Second, you will cut all ties to the Racub brothers."

"That's ridiculous," Clement said.

"They're the chief funders of the Rapture Party. We wouldn't last two minutes. The voters would drive us out of office. And your request that I leave the country—that Whites, Yellows and Blacks leave the country, it'll never happen. Moreover, your sale of my soul to this—this Hobomock is invalid. I declare it null and void."

"But, my lease on your soul was three years." The Devil protested.

Clement shoved the Letter of Agreement toward the Devil.

"Did you look at the date?" The Devil looked at the Letter of Agreement. It had expired the day before.

"I owe you nothing," Clement said.

"Moreover, a White House lawyer said that the part of the agreement was worded incorrectly. Get out and take this stinking savage with you."

Turning to the Devil, Hobomock said. "You mean you messed up the agreement? Francis was right. You are too polite."

"Yes, well I'll let you two sort things out among yourselves. Now if you gentlemen will excuse me," Clement said.

Hobomock said: "You beat me this time Jones, but I'm not finished with you yet. I'll get you. I just need some more time."

Hobomock, called "the god of low places," was so angry that he turned into a huge black snake that slithered down the stairs and out of the building. The Devil left the White House and headed for a travel agency.

Chapter 29

The imposter Black Peter was exposed when the Spirit of Black Peter showed up and began performing miracles. At first, he tried to take credit for them, but was finally found out. He tried to steer the NIX to worship Haile Selassie but Boy Bishop had enough supporters in the sect to crush the revolt. Threatened by what he considered a hostile takeover by a fake Rastafarian whom the Rastafarian elite had never heard of. Without the funds available to him as a member of the Nicolaites, as a result of Boy Bishop's contacts with his rich friends, the imposter Black Peter was broke. But after a coke mule was murdered, he took his place and even had some people working under him. He had risen to become a Baron who went by the name of Sleigh Ride. He threw great parties. He was sitting on a throne-like chair in his expensive uptown apartment overlooking the East River. His guests were dancing and singing Cham's song.

Listen mi nuh babylon bwoy, babylon bwoy, babylon bwoooooooyyy!!!

No mi nuh Babylon bwoy, babylon bwoy, babylon bwoooooooyyy!!!

*Hear mi now babylon bwoy, babylon bwoy, babylon
bwooooooyyy!!!*

*Mek mi tell yuh somethin babylon bwoy, babylon
bwoy*

Babylon bwoooooooyyy!!!!

They were having a good time. Lavish buffet. People
in some of the upstairs bedrooms fucking. Mounds
of dopamine boosters. A bar whose bartender could
mix any drink requested. Nude swimming in the outdoor rooftop swimming pool. The door was broken
down and in charged some police followed by Police
Commissioner Brown and Mayor Loathsome Larry.
The two were all out of breath. Larry ordered everybody out of the place which was followed by people
trampling over each other for the exit. "Cuff him,"
Brown instructed one of the policemen, while another
was sweeping some of the coke into a cellophane bag.
Sleigh Ride was dragged out of the apartment screaming about his constitutional rights and demanding to
see his lawyer. The Mayor ordered the policeman who
was carrying the bag full of coke to hand it over to him.
"But this has to go to the crime lab," the policeman said.
Brown snatched the bag from the policeman's hand. The
police left, leaving Brown and the mayor alone. They
started passing the coke around and spooning it. After
one snort the Mayor said, "This is some good shit."

Chapter 30

Wham. Sleigh Ride fell from his chair. His handcuffs were on too tight. His mouth was full of blood where he'd been smacked. Police Commissioner Brown had his shirt sleeves rolled up.

"I told you that I don't know."

"We can do this the hard way, bring in the water boarding equipment," Brown said. That was the cue for the mayor to come in.

"Police Commissioner Brown, what on earth are you doing to this man?"

"I'm trying to get him to tell us where his buddies are hiding. Those fucking Nicolaites."

"Commissioner Brown, this is no way to treat a prisoner."

"You want me to leave?" Brown asked, winking at Larry.

Smiling as he approached Sleigh Ride, the mayor hummed, "*Time to separate the pros from the cons/ the platinum from the bronze.* Let me handle this," Loathsome said to Brown with a wink.

Wow, Sleigh Ride thought. *The fucking mayor, Loathsome Larry, the guy who came to fame by blowing away a bunch of players, quoting Jay Z. Maybe I had him all wrong.*

"Suit yourself," Brown said, exiting.

"Smoke?"

"Yessir, I need one." The mayor pulled out a joint.

"What?" Sleigh Ride said. "I thought that you meant cigarettes."

"This is the modern NYPD. We have to be groovy with the times." They smoked for a while. Corresponding silently. Breaking into giggles from time to time. Finally, the mayor said. "You hungry?" Sleigh Ride, grinning, nodded his head. A cop brought in a New York steak, mashed potatoes topped with gravy, green peas, salad, and a beer. Sleigh Ride dug in. When he finished, he was brought a dessert. Ice cream topped with strawberries.

"Now, Sleigh Ride, you have to give me the address of the Nicolaites. Or else I have to bring Police Commissioner Brown back."

"But I'd be identified as a snitch?"

"Maybe we can make a deal. Plus, you don't have any allegiance to Boy Bishop. Besides he threw you out."

"That's true but if I tell you, if I snitch, my life on the streets would be worthless."

"OK," the mayor said. He asked the policeman to fetch Commissioner Brown. "Bring in the waterboarding equipment."

"Wait. Wait. I'll give you the address of their headquarters."

The mayor examined the address.

"So, what do I get in exchange for this information?"

"You won't get any jail time." Sleigh Ride was so relieved that he almost kissed the mayor.

"But you have to cut us in on 80 percent of your Snow sales," the police commissioner said.

"But that leaves nothing for me."

"We'll send you to Sing Sing and tell all of your homies that you're a rat."

"OK... I... I accept." After signing an agreement of cooperation, Loathsome said, "Get him the fuck out of here," with a wave of his hand. After they'd taken Sleigh Ride away, Brown came in and gave Larry a fist bump. They and SWAT entered a brownstone in the West Village. The address that had been given to him by Sleigh Ride. There were signs that the Nicolaites had been there, but had left in a hurry. Christmas ornaments were up. A painting of Nicholas with the Bacchus wreath around his head. The food was still warm on an elaborate dining room table. The SWAT team left the mayor and the police commissioner alone. They sat down at the table and finished the meal.

Communique from The Nix.

Chapter 31

Boy Bishop and his associates were sending out a communique. He was seated. Like the others, he was wearing a mask. Standing behind him were armed men and women. Boy Bishop said, "It came between the planet and Chuck and Chuck lost. Scientists have tried to warn earthlings of the extinction that faces us and they have failed to communicate. The media, which receives billions in advertising from gas guzzlers, present both sides of the debate. What debate? We will end the debate by warning all of those who benefit from removing fossils from the ground that what happened to Chuck will happen to them. They will join the source of their profits in the ground. The only answer to this crisis is monarchy. A green philosopher King like the one recommended by Plato. Someone who will keep the fossil fuels in the ground. The earth is too precious to leave its fate in the hands of democratic rule. It is time for the stabilizing hand to return. The monarchy. Not one with the usual regal trappings, the court, a crown-wearing King, and much ceremony, but a Green monarch, who will keep oil and coal where God sent them. Democracy has failed. How else would you explain the Hatch government, a Rev. Clement Jones, who has become a billionaire while working in government? And now a man, Termite Control, a worshiper of Odin and someone whose idea of lovemaking is disgusting. Can a monarchy be worse?"

The communique ended. Nance Saturday learned little from the video, but his spider part learned a lot. His uncle told him that he was named after the original Spider Man, Anansi. What his uncle left out was that his relationship to Anansi went beyond that.

Chapter 32

His uncle had summoned him. He had been raised by his uncle because his mother, a teenager when she gave birth to him, was incapable of caring for him. That was the story. When he entered the four-story Brooklyn brownstone, the three "mothers" who were in a polyamorous relationship and who helped raise him greeted him affectionately. One took his coat and another called up to his uncle who had converted the fourth floor into a gym. He had read that exercise wards off neuro degeneration. His uncle told him to meet him in his library located on the second floor.

Before exercising, the old man had probably been at his computer, probably writing an abstract for a conference he would be attending. From the window of the library, which was lined with books, one could see all the way down to Wall Street. He stood up slowly and embraced Nance. In the embrace, Nance could tell that the uncle had fragile bones, despite the exercise. Possibly Osteoporosis. His doctor recommended 2000 mg of vitamin D. "I'm very proud of you, Nance."

"Imagine, traveling to the Vatican not only to meet with the pope, but enjoy his hospitality. A Black pope at that. I lived to see a Black pope.

"It was an interesting experience," Nance said.

"He seems bent upon cleaning the church of its evil and decadence, but he has to be cautious. He saw what happened to his predecessor, who attracted the hatred of the more conservative elements in the Church. Successors to those who began the Inquisition led by this Cardinal called Adrien."

"Yes, it was horrid what happened to his predecessor, but this thing about copycat devils preventing him from entering the Vatican and his having to temporarily live at the Summer Palace is nonsense. I'm a man of science and I find such things to be humbug."

"A writer named Ishmael Reed said in 1974 that the Church was full of the Devil. He had a premonition. The abuse scandals didn't surface until the 1980s."

"How do you suppose he guessed that? Is he some kind of Nostradamus?"

"He says that the best people whom he ever knew, Lois Cunningham, a former nun, and Ted Cunningham a former priest, left the Church. He figured that something must have been wrong. James Joyce, when he wrote about the decadence of the Irish Church, must have known, too. Pope Francis said that the Devil was outside of the Church busily seducing Bishops but, like the movie, *When a Stranger Calls*, a 1979 American psychological horror film, they didn't realize that copycat devils were in the Vatican. The devils were in the house. And now the Vatican's evil has burst and the little devils can be seen sitting and grinning at the top of the dome. Miltiades II can't move into the Vatican until this mass hallucination subsides."

"Well, this merely means that irrationality has swept the planet." There was a pause.

"Do you know why I called you here?"

"No, uncle."

"Nance, I've had a full productive life. My articles have been published in over 500 peer review professional journals, I have received numerous awards for my scientific achievement and I have this four-story Federal style house here in Brooklyn. And watching you grow has brought me great satisfaction. But all of my wealth—the maid, the cook, your mothers—all of these luxuries are the result of a bad contract. A contract that earned me millions."

"I don't follow, Uncle."

"Of course, I wanted you to go to college, but you seem to be doing well living by your wits. That limousine service. Since even college graduates were having a hard time getting jobs, waiting tables and driving Uber and Lyft—you said that you wanted to be self-employed. That if you punched in 9-5 it would be a waste of time. That you'd always suffer the agony of watching the clock. You were determined to be your own boss."

"I had to end it because of Uber and Lyft. I'm devoting full time to being a troubleshooter."

"Nance, let me give you some background. You know about Entomology."

"Yes, the study of insects."

"Would it surprise you that insects have been used in warfare for over 5000 years? In fact, more soldiers have died from diseases spread by insects than by bullets. In fact, there is a saying, 'The proboscis proved mightier than the sword.'"

"Uncle, what does that have to do with me?"

"You've been lucky so far. Nobody has sprayed you with Black Flag. Just kiddin."

An odd remark. Must be dementia settling in, Nance thought.

"You're like a Siamese twin, only your twin is a spider."

"What?"

"Nance, as a young person my research showed that spiders and humans have a common ancestor. They found evidence of this common ancestor in China. The Chengjiang formation. My team and I traveled there and extracted some DNA from this fossil. It was thought that these fossils were so old that it would be impossible to find traces of DNA. But Dinosaur blood cells were extracted from a 75-million-year-old fossil. We...." He began to sob.

"We injected some of its DNA into your embryo."

"You what!!!!" Nance started toward his uncle who had taken a seat.

"You were to be mostly man but sprinkled with a little spider."

"How did this happen? Why me?"

"Nance, the story that we told you was made up. I'm not your uncle and there was no sister who was incapable of caring for you. With a research grant, we hired a woman who was desperate for some quick cash. We artificially impregnated her and she carried you for those nine months."

"You mean I was born as a result of an experiment? You're just now telling me this?"

"Nance, didn't it occur to you that when you were in high school you wrote about spiders as your science project? And that in English class, you were fascinated by that Robert Lowell poem, 'Mr. Edwards and the Spider'? That you were an addict of TV runs of the 50s show, 'The Web'? You would stay up late at night to watch movies, like *Tarantula*, *Eight Legged Freaks*, *Earth vs. the Spider*. You couldn't wait for *National Geographic* documentaries. Why do you think I named you Nance, after Anansi, and provided you with books about this trickster? Indications are that the spider gene will lie dormant. It would have turned on by now. The good news is that the experiment has obviously failed."

"But the spider gene has turned on. I took the shape of a spider at the Vatican. I thought that it was a dream. I was able to hear some conservative cardinals discussing a plot against the Black pope. Led by Adrien, a Spanish Cardinal. Uncle, how could you do this to me?

"What do you suggest I do?" Nance asked.

"I have some pills. When you feel this transformation taking place, swallow these pills." He handed Nance a bottle. Nance accepted it. Nance was trembling. Angry.

"But why?" Nance asked.

"Nance, the Pentagon said that if we created humans who could become spiders, they would make very efficient spies. Superior to carrier pigeons, less expensive than drones. You could also arm insects with nuclear weapons. They're now working on some so tiny that they could be attached to a mosquito's legs."

"You still haven't answered my question. Why did you do it?"

"I was ambitious."

"What!!" Nance rose to leave. "I don't think that I'll be coming around anymore. Uncle, I'm disappointed in you. I really admired you."

"Nance, take the pills. Maybe it isn't too late."

Nance walked out into the hall.

"Nance, please forgive me." Nance didn't respond. He turned away from his "uncle" in disgust and walked toward the door. His "uncle" broke down. He was having a hard time catching his breath. A skinny White dude entered the room carrying a portable oxygen tent. He put the mask over his uncle's face.

The White dude, Andrew, his husband whom he had met at a Greenwich Village bar a few months before, laced into Nance. "How could you do this to him? He clothed you and gave you the best education. Sent you to the best private schools. And what did you do with it? Driving a gypsy limousine and giving advice to chiselers who don't want to pay their way. With your math skills you could have worked on Wall Street. NASA. The Vatican even asked you to help with their books. No wonder your wife Virginia left you. She didn't want to spend her life with a loser."

Nance didn't respond. He turned away from his "uncle" and his "uncle's" husband. He walked into the hall, where one of the women who had raised him stood. "You knew about this?" She shook her head, sadly. It occurred to him that his three mothers might be government scientists assigned to observe the experiment, which was him. He walked out slamming the door behind him and into the noisy, busy New York streets.

Chapter 33

They met in a bar in Harlem. Her chauffeur parked the car in front. She ordered a Scotch on the rocks. She looked at the menu. They settled on appetizers. She had a salad and squid. He ordered crab cakes. They agreed that he would email her about every development.

She said, curtly, "What do you have for me, Mr. Saturday?"

"I've had a breakthrough. I think I can find answers, but it will involve some extra-legal methods. It might involve a kidnapping." His mouth was moving but it wasn't his words. In fact, he sounded an octave lower than his usual voice.

"Kidnapping?"

"I think I have a lead. I'll email you about my progress. I'll find the headquarters of the Nicolaites. And turn them in." Again. It wasn't even his voice.

"Your methods are superior to those of Mayor Loathsome Larry and Police Commissioner Brown."

"I'll tell you where the NIX are hiding and you can tell them. I don't want them to know that I was the source of the information. Look at any film noir. There's always a conflict between the police and private eyes. I don't want those two on my back."

"I'll send you a nice check and a bonus if you succeed."

"I agree with the goals of the Nicolaites. But they're going about it the wrong way. Those people at Racub Fossil Fuel Industry are reasonable. If one would show them the scientific evidence, they'd probably end fracking. Besides, we don't need a monarchy. We fought against King George for our freedom."

What was he saying? Was he one of those two heads that you see in African art? Only his other head was that of a spider. His lips were moving but it wasn't him.

"So true." She shook his hand and left. Then he asked one of the waiters the direction to the restroom.

Chapter 34

When Boy Bishop read his communique, Nance's human eye had noticed Boy Bishop's clothing, the blue gown and the pendant he wore, a silver boat, symbol of the NIX. It referred to one of the Saint's miracles. Some sailors were grounded and Saint Nicolas rescued them. Nance's human side heard his statement, noticed the accent and the speaker's gestures. But unbeknownst to Nance, his eight spider's eyes noticed a termite in a wall behind the Nicolaites. Later his Anansi side waited until the Queen appeared within her entourage of foot soldiers, her armed escorts. The thing about Anansi is that while other animals had to chase or find their food, all that he had to do was spin a web and wait. As soon as they approached where Anansi was hidden, his twin grabbed her. Her escorts tried to save her, but it was too late. She was now in his orbit. Later Anansi sent a message that he would release her after negotiations. They finally got back to Nance with the location of the NIX hideout. They had no choice. They needed their queen in order to survive.

Chapter 35

His ex-wife, Virginia, who was now an executive producer at KCAK, heard about his meeting with the pope. She picked Nance up and took him to dinner at a restaurant located on the first floor of a popular Central Park hideaway. He was standing in the wet snow. The day before, it was 100 degrees. She finally arrived. Late. She was in the backseat of a Cadillac SUV. The driver opened the door for them to exit. She put her arm in his as they entered the restaurant.

This was the kind of place where if you pulled out a cigarette thirty waiters would show up to light it. When the Maître D looked up at her, his face lit up. He started bowing and scraping. "Welcome, Mrs. Saturday," and things like that. As they walked to their table all of the diners noticed her and began whispering. They were seated.

"Nance, I can't believe that you would accept money from such a woman. A gold digger. What on earth could she be doing for you? I'll bet I know."

"She wasn't after his money. They had a mutual interest in art. She chose the art for his many homes." Their conversation kept being interrupted by film and media stars, coming over to the table to greet her. Her iPhone kept buzzing.

"Besides, I needed the money. Uber and Lyft replaced my limousine service. I got weary of ducking airport cops as I tried to pick up arriving passengers. She hired me as a troubleshooter. I was recommended by the pope. They were friends when he was a cardinal here in New York."

"But it reflects badly on me. My reputation. Your being connected to a woman who married a man for his money. I still bear your name. That slut? She has all of the aesthetics of a peppermint stick. I'll bet you're fucking her too. Now that your Russian bitch returned to Moscow." She always brought up the Russian bitch. After they separated, he'd had an affair with a Russian mathematician. They'd met when he attended a lecture of hers where she responded to Claudia Zaslavsky's article "Mathematics of the Yoruba People and of Their Neighbors in Southern Nigeria."

The waiter came with the wine list. She ordered an expensive glass of Mondavi Family Estate Premiere Napa Valley Red. He ordered coffee. "You're still nursing a grudge about my success," she said. More silence. He looked up as a movie star and his entourage walked in. He was one of these American actors who, having great success, hadn't made any effort to improve his skills. Hadn't earned his success by undergoing the rigors of training like British actors. Coasted along on the basis of his looks. She didn't pay any attention. Seeing Virginia, he came to their table and began bowing and scraping with even a deeper bow than the Maître D.

The women with him looked on in awe. His agent was begging for an interview. Virginia handed her her card. Noticing the chill with which she was greeting them, he and his coterie moved to their reserved table, but once in a while Nance noticed them looking over at their table. Virginia returned to fingering the keyboard on her smartphone. Without looking up she said: "Nance, I want you to get me an interview with the pope."

"O, that's why you invited me to lunch. The answer is no. How could you ask me such a thing?"

"But, Nance," She leaned over and while doing so revealed those great glorious Black mounds. They'd been divorced for a while but he still had fantasies about those mounds. Mounds that he once crawled all over. Mounds he used to reach the pinnacle of like he was Sir Edmund Hillary or somebody. He was one of the last men in America to notice the beauty of a woman's body. Most men were scared to compliment women. Songs, poetry and art had become unisexual.

"I'll see what I can do," he said, weakly. She leaned back and became business-like again.

"So how are things going, generally, Nance?"

"Working for Chuck's widow is keeping me away from the breadlines."

"I'll bet."

"It's all professional. Besides why are you concerned about who I'm sharing the sack with? You said that I was a bad lover."

"You were not a bad lover, just hungry. Overwhelming. I felt sometimes as though you had six hands." She was lying. Even after their divorce, she'd show up at his door, usually after some corporate party and spend the night with him. They'd go at it. He would make that holler like Lightnin' Hopkins makes during his songs. Sometimes when they came together, he thought he heard her speaking in tongues. When he brought up these nocturnal habits of hers, she'd say she didn't remember or that she'd had too much to drink.

"A lot of women say that they enjoy someone who could cover every erogenous zone."

"They must be freaks like you."

The waiter came with the check. Virginia laid one of those black credit cards on the receipt. The one reserved for VIPs. Nance looked up to see a familiar face. A famous Hollywood producer. His lawyers were keeping him away from the women who said that he'd made advances even after they'd said no. Nance wondered how many had said yes. There were a number of White men who were prominent in film and television who'd been accused of making inappropriate moves toward women. They were still working. Virginia had lent her name to a film of his, which convinced the distributors that it was worth investing in. It was one of those Black-on-Black crime numbers for which mall audiences have an insatiable appetite. They began chatting as though he wasn't there. He took their being absorbed in conversation as an opportunity to leave. He was still hungry. He found himself on a subway headed downtown. He ended up at 50 Spring Street. The Antojeria Popular. He ordered an Ant Burger. He pigged out. An Ant Burger? He ate three. How did he get here, a place with which he was unfamiliar?

Chapter 36

He got a Tiffany thank you card from Virginia accompanied by a Tiffany vase. He had contacted Pope Miltiades II, his friend, and set up her interview. He watched the interview on television. Miltiades was showing her around the Summer Palace. He could see that they admired each other. They were cooing and carrying on. He got so turned off, he changed the channel.

Thousands were continuing to converge on Washington. They wanted to be in the vicinity of the White House where the miracle had occurred. All of the hotels were booked for two years. People didn't mind if they had to settle for suburban hotels and motels. Homeowners were making money from short term bookings. The Governor of New Jersey ordered the Highway Patrol to protect the Trenton home where Bob Krantz was born. His father, who was a dentist and his mother, who was an accountant, now lived in Florida. A mountain of flowers stood before their suburban ranch styled home. Hundreds gathered at night, singing hymns and lighting candles. Scavengers were looting his home. Anything, an ashtray or a soap dish, was bringing in big prices at Sotheby's.

Chapter 37

The Left Hand Path, an international conglomerate made up of trillionaires and billionaires, had taken over an entire Swiss castle located high up in the Alps for their meeting. There was an abundance of food laid out in a buffet. Ladies. Entertainment. All had been arranged by a staff which took the names of biblical apostles as their email monikers.

There were multinational CEOs, sheiks, emirs, and other fossil fuel moguls. They were still laughing over a skit by a comedian that poked fun at the slow pace of NASA's space exploration, which for them was an example of what happens when you depend upon the government instead of the private sector. After an intermission, the 500 or so members of the Path got down to serious business. One of their scientists was about to reveal the progress of a top-secret space program. There was much chattering as he mounted the stage in the ballroom of this 16th-century castle.

He was introduced to enthusiastic applause. He finally made a signal for the audience to quiet down. He began his speech by pointing to the wretched condition of the planet and its terrifying future. Of refugees seeking water, food and shelter. Of wars over the simple needs of humans. Coastal cities underwater. Pandemonium. Already island nations were disappearing as hurricanes were becoming deadlier. The scientist (who could be played by Anthony Hopkins or John Malkovich), talked about their attempts to manage world governments through bribes only to have them run by miscreants and dullards. How their attempt to weed out the genetically damaged, making more room for their people, had failed. Oxygen grabbers. Surplus people. That the only solution was to abandon a dying planet. Then came the stunner. They discovered the technology that would enable them to reach the Goldilocks planet of Dido. Because global warming caused the melting of a glacier, they discovered a spaceship that had crashed thousands of years ago and was buried under the ice. It was located by a crew hired by a billionaire, who had been seeking new opportunities to become even richer by using new trade routes made possible by the disappearance of the ice. He had the ship sent secretly to scientists employed by The Left Hand. The origin of the spaceship was unknown.

The Pentagon was no longer dismissing flying saucers as illusions. They existed. Dismantling the spaceship, scientists employed by the LHP had found an energy source unknown to Earthlings. They decoded maps they found on board, of shortcuts to a planet that the inhabitants called Dido. Using this ship as a model, the LHP had built five hundred of these saucers. The scientist promised, "We're now ready to lift off to the stars. It will only take a year to reach the planet.

The average age of the men on board will be sixty. The average age of the women will be twenty-three." This last remark was greeted with great enthusiasm. Some of the members of the audience began to hug one another.

"Gentlemen," the host continued, "I know that you regret leaving this planet, the home for you and your ancestors, but this group, the NIX, is making life miserable for you and others. They've gone international. These assassins are killing our people whose only crime is bringing progress to the world."

"Hear, hear," echoed some of the audience members.

"Where would we be without oil, coal and our new technology, fracking," another said.

"How could our fellow Earthlings be more ungrateful? You," the speaker said, pointing to a Texas billionaire, "They spurned your beneficence. Your contributing to symphony orchestras, museums. And you, Sheik, using your billions to build a magnificent city in the middle of the desert. It's not your fault that there are more vacancies than occupied condos and office buildings." The Sheik was known globally as someone who dismembered or poisoned his enemies, including members of the press. He was consulted by tyrants all over the world for his expertise on ethnic cleansing. He owned half the real estate in New York, which he was trying to sell. The Island of Manhattan was about to join other coastal cities underwater.

The Sheik stood. "The poor line up and I greet them, seated in a humble tent, and I give them five dollars apiece each year. They are so ungrateful. Some of our members have defected. Putting billions into renewable energy sources. One big hoax. Windmills and such. As for me, النفط والفحم إلى الأبد which in English means, 'Oil and Coal forever.'" Members of The Left Hand stood and applauded.

"Exactly. None of us is safe. We must stick together. Chuck with all of his protection, his security, couldn't escape these assassins led by the maniac Boy Bishop. It is definitely time to leave," the scientist said.

They all agreed and prepared for takeoff. They set the date to a year from the day of their meeting. Members of the Path began to depart the Great Hall for their private planes, leaving the staff, whose emails bore the names of the 12 apostles, to begin a report to be sent to those members who couldn't attend. But suddenly a ball like object rolled across the entrance to the hall blocking their exit. The guests looked on in horror. It was Chuck's head. Alarms went off and the building was surrounded but the NIX responsible for the deed had escaped.

Part 2

Chapter 38

Nance hadn't contacted J.Q. since he'd returned from Rome. He decided to make a visit. She now lived in an apartment located near Spring Street. He climbed the steps toward her apartment. One of the White ethnics, who'd resisted the gentrification, peeked out from behind her door. The door to her apartment was ajar. He walked in. Momentarily, he heard someone singing in between another person making groans and moans. The sounds were coming from the bedroom. He walked toward the door and peeked in. J.Q. was naked, the palms of her hands pressed against the bed. Her lover had entered her from behind. They both seemed to be enjoying themselves. This death squad leader that she had been dating was singing while balling her. He'd heard the song before. They played it at the United Nations party, when he and his entourage entered the room (T3s). He was singing their song and waving his country's flag as he was fucking J.Q. Nance shook his head and left the apartment. As he reached the final landing, some men rushed by him. They could have been extras in the *Scarface* movies. He walked out into the street. Had a cup of espresso at a coffee shop near 8th Avenue. Shortly, he heard sirens. They were heading in his direction. Later, he learned on the news that his enemies had murdered J.Q.'s lover just as he had finished making love to J.Q. and was putting on his shorts.

Chapter 39

After Chuck's widow informed Mayor Loathsome and Police Commissioner Brown of the NIX hideout, they headed toward the location. Pretty soon the upstate barn where they plotted their nefarious deeds was surrounded. The mayor remained in the car while Brown led the police into the hiding place. Soon they were marching NIX out of the barn, their hands up. But where was Boy Bishop?

"I'll check downstairs." Brown told the other cops. He descended to the basement and began his search. He found Bishop hiding. Seeing Brown, Bishop arose and turned around for Brown to cuff him. Brown looked at him and grinned. B.B. waited. He turned around again. Brown had returned to the upstairs loft of the barn. Boy Bishop heard him say. "No trace of him down there." Bishop opened a basement window and fled.

Chapter 40

Ice Cream was in terrible pain at the site of the amputa-
tion. It was night. He broke into a pharmacy and found
painkillers. He swallowed them. He'd gone through the
two thousand dollars and had to find some money. He
needed to go to Glock's and ask him to announce to
the public that this was a stunt that had gone bad. Ice
Cream's mansion was guarded by a security firm hired
by Gladiola. He'd left it to her in his will and so she
now occupied it. He couldn't go there. He had picked
up some clothes from various donation stations around
Manhattan where used clothes had been deposited. He
took some money from the pharmacy's cash register.
The alarm went off. He heard the sirens. He took off.
Finally, he boarded the train to Long Island where
Glock's estate was located. He then took a cab from the
station to Glock's. Glock's mansion was a duplicate of
the one seen in *Scarface*. A 10,000-square-foot house
surrounded by 10 acres of Persian gardens, pools, and
patios, the kind with Byzantine-inspired barrel-vaulted
ceilings, beautiful tilework. Ice Cream knew his way
around, having visited Glock's home many times. The
front door of the mansion was open. He heard some

men talking. He walked into the room. The walls were covered with framed posters advertising James Bond movies. Glock was having a meeting with his men. Seeing Ice Cream, the men pulled their guns. The sound of clicks. Glock placed the bottle of champagne from which he had been swigging on a table. Glock told his men to lower their guns. Glock was wearing a red Tallia jacket, red pants designed by Grace Wales Bonner, and Manolo Blahnik sandals.

"Who the fuck are you?" Glock asked.

"Ice Cream. Don't you recognize me?"

"Ice Cream is dead. He was killed by a mugger."

"But don't you remember. It was supposed to be a joke. I put on the blackface so the politically correct crowd would protest, and I'd apologize—"

"If that's true, why is it still on your face? You would have wiped it off. Besides, Ice Cream didn't have no one arm, did he boys?" The men agreed, laughing.

"That's because I was shot! The makeup artist who applied the blackface was an imposter. The real one said that she was late. I think the fake makeup artist put some kind of witchcraft on me. I can't take it off."

The men laughed, some holding their sides. A couple sinking to the floor and rolling over. Glock, laughing himself, said, "Get this crazy motherfucker out of here." The men, still laughing, drove Ice Cream to the entrance of the estate and threw him out. Out of options, Ice Cream decided that there was only one remaining place where he'd be accepted.

Chapter 41

In her email, Mrs. Chuck asked Nance how he got ahold
of the information. He said, he'd rather not say. If he
had told her that termites gave him the information
in exchange for freeing their queen, she'd thought he
was crazy. With the check that she gave him, the days
of doing odd jobs were over for Nance. He could con-
centrate on full time troubleshooting work. In fact, he
threw away the pills that his uncle gave him. Pills that
would have expelled his spider side. He was like Lamont
Cranston. He had an extra weapon, unlike others in his
field. In her email, she requested a meeting. When he
arrived at a coffee shop in the Village, he found her sitting outside. She was accompanied by a large Black man
with robust facial features and a work-out body. They
were introduced. Nance ordered a double espresso.

"Nance, this is Charles. He's someone whom I call
upon when a job needs some heavy lifting. He will be
your partner."

"Hey, Bro." He stuck out his huge Black hand. He
had a deep voice like Barry White. Rich people have
enforcers like this. When Truman Capote revealed their
secrets, they had him beaten up. Underneath a blue

overcoat, he wore a black scarf, white shirt, red tie, a black pin striped suit and hat. Brown cordovan shoes. He looked like the anti-hero of a noir novel.

"Help in doing what, may I ask?"

"Have you heard the story that Dean Clift's entourage (T.3s) disappeared on the way to the Capitol after Justice Nola Payne cast the vote declaring his removal from office unconstitutional?"

"That's what they say," Nance said.

"Someone emailed me a map, which shows where he and his associates are located. The emailer said that he was leaving for Europe and wanted to get this off his conscience." He gave Nance the map.

"What would you have me do?"

"I want you to free Dean Clift and bring him back to Washington. I have a personal reason for requesting this mission. You see," she paused, sighed and said: "Dean Clift is my father."

Nance thought to himself: *It was rumored that Dean had had sex with 3000 women. How many more would be coming forth?*

"He met my mother at a party when he was a congressman."

Charles and Nance decided to depart the next morning. They would use one of his two airport limousines for the trip. A classic Lincoln Continental. And they'd be on their way. Charles would read the map directions while Nance drove. But first, Nance had to execute an intervention.

Chapter 42

Nance heard the news on his smartphone. The NIX were being frog marched out of their hideout. It was a motley group. Asians, Latinx, LGBTQ, Blacks, Native-Americans, et al., all dedicated to saving the oceans. Boy Bishop, according to the report, had escaped. Nance was being shown his new office at the top floor of an office building in Manhattan. He could see both the Hudson and the East Rivers. His spider's brain had out-smarted his human brain. His spider part with its eight eyes could see what his human two eyes failed to see. Humans who believe that they are the greatest among all sentient beings do not realize that all life is sentient. Having spotted the termite behind Boy Bishop when he sent the communique, the spider in Nance noticed the termite crawling across a wall behind him. And so Nance's spider side waited until the army and its queen were making a crossing. He flew down and swooped up the queen. The generals tried to rescue her, but Nance threatened them with his venom. He told them that he would release her if they would direct them to Boy Bishop's headquarters. They declined. They said that they were not permitted to engage in human affairs.

All that humans could do for them was to provide them with some wood. And so he held their queen hostage. At first, she resisted. But then she began to enjoy his stickiness which at first repelled her. She loved rolling around in his silk bed and flying thru the air holding on to him as though she was on the back of a bike with her arms around the waist of the driver.

Finally, the army yielded. Without her they couldn't reproduce. She didn't want to leave, especially when he told her that she was more beautiful than the Termite Queen who appeared in *Wonder Woman* #58 (March/April 1953). But in the end, she chose duty over love. He texted the direction of the NIX hideout to his sponsor who passed it onto Mayor Loathsome Larry.

Chapter 43

Nance had called a Lyft to take him to a restaurant where he'd told J.Q. to meet him. The car was there within minutes. Yellow Cabs were complaining about Lyft and Uber crowding them out of business, but after decades of humiliating Black people for refusing to provide them with service, Nance figured that this was Karma. They drove through downtown Manhattan. He got out of the car and entered the restaurant. Momentarily, J.Q. walked in and sat down. She had been working for a small Brooklyn paper, which had gone under as the Digitalites sought news on their iPhones and tablets. She went to acting school and had gotten roles in the classic theater—Shakespeare, Shaw's Saint Joan. There were many scripts by Black playwrights available, but the American theater had become devoted to the bottom line, as much as publishing, and so producers felt that these plays would annoy or even outrage those who could afford to buy tickets. She was now an actress and so had practiced a walk that was hers alone. As though she was carrying a pitcher of water on her head. She was from the Caribbean and so had seen many women walking that walk in the marketplace. She had mastered the swish. In Carnival, the women have their bodies do the talking. She saw him sitting in a booth and joined him. She kissed him on the cheek. They engaged in some small talk. How was your trip to Rome? What have you been up to? They finally got down to business.

"I want you to come work for me. I have a rich client who will lead me to more. I've already bought space in a midtown building. We'll work there. It has a view of both the East and Hudson rivers."

She laughed. "I'm an actress. My job is on the stage. Before cameras."

"Yeah, but this is not the time for actresses with your complexion. The trend is dark energy. After decades of being excluded, even in movies filmed by Black producers, Black women are in. That old expression has come to fruition. The blacker the berry, the sweeter the juice. They are appearing on the cover of magazines, have leading roles in movies. Vanessa Williams has been replaced by Viola Davis. Humans are getting back to basics."

"You're asking me to give up my career and come work for you."

"What career? You're getting older. Even White actresses have a hard time getting roles when they age. How do you think it's going to be for you? And your choice in men?"

"That's none of your goddamn business, Nance."

"What about this death squad leader? You could have been killed when those assassins murdered him. And then the crazy motherfucker who took hostages at the supermarket, the scoundrel that you moved into your apartment only for you to discover that he'd escaped from Rikers Island and then that Nigerian who was arrested for running a fake lottery—"

"Those men were wounded during their childhood. They're suffering from post-traumatic stress. This is why they made wrong choices—I was helping in their transformation. Their recovery."

"That's some silly shit." There was a pause, "I need for you to let me know by Monday, whether you want the job."

"O so you're going to give me orders, tell me whom to date, and then give me an ultimatum. You're such a fucking patriarch, Nance. I don't have to take this from you, Nance."

"I need for you to let me know by Monday, whether you want the job."

The waiter came with the menu. Glancing at the menu J.Q. grabbed her face. Her mouth opened in a state of shock.

"Is this some kind of joke?"

"What joke? Grasshopper fries, Ant Burgers. They're delicious." The other voice took over.

"You're crazy." She got up and rushed from the restaurant. Never mind. After he finished his meal of barbecued caterpillar, he began to walk toward the East River, but noticed a crowd gathered around a news vending machine. He saw the headlines in the newspaper that had been installed in the vending machine. The headlines were set in the kind of screaming fonts that were used in the times of warfare.

Pope Marries Virginia Saturday, Bombshell Rocks the Catholic Church. College of Cardinals in Emergency Session.

The pope acknowledged in a tweet. "God is no Einstein and so he proves he exists through love."

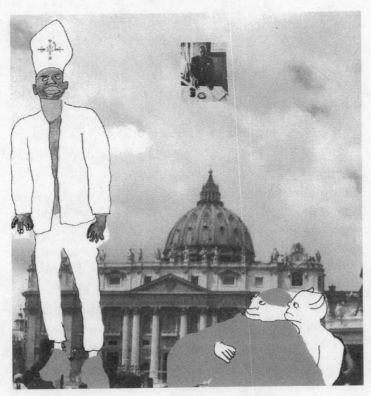

The Black Pope and his enemy, Cardinal Adrien, and the Cardinal's advisor.

Chapter 44

There had been a lot of changes among the White House staff. Esther had retired to Louisiana. She was living on her Social Security and pension. Joan had died from complications due to breast cancer. John's grandson had become a congressman. He would quit his job at the White House as soon as he finished his memoirs about working in the White House during the Jones/Hatch years. After he finished his meal, he returned to writing.

"Today, the Devil came to present his demands to Jones. He was accompanied by a man who was dressed like an Indian who goes by the name of Hobomock. Looks like this Hobomock had turned the tables on the Devil. During the Devil's stopover in New York, the Devil told Jones that his soul was now the property of Hobomock, but Jones pointed to the Letter of Agreement, to show that his lease on Jones' soul had expired the day before. This Hobomock was really flustered. He was there to order Jones to begin the exodus of Blacks and Whites from America and that he would return the Devil back to Europe where he was created. That whale who died from eating garbage really got to Hobomock. Hobomock and the Wampanoag had a white whale myth before Melville's ancestors had any idea that America existed. Hobomock wanted Whites and the Blacks, the Browns and the Yellows to go back to where they came from. He delivered his demands. His argument was that the idea that after the triumph of Christianity the Devil and his followers fled to America was false history. It was the Europeans who brought the Devil to America and it was up to the Europeans to return him to his home. The household was missing the old days when the only haunts were Lincoln, Dolly Madison and Andrew Jackson. Now the place had been haunted by Heinrich, the ghost that stowed away on Air Force One after Reagan's trip to Bitburg where he honored the SS dead. He became one of Clement's advisers. The Devil made him get rid of him. I remember Heinrich's complaint when he was asked to leave the Oval Office. *Du Hast Mich Betrogen*!!! Rumors had it that Heinrich was now working for Termite Control. The same for Joe Beowulf, the robot that dealt with Clement's enemies. Followers of Termite Control had found the junk yard where he'd been left and reassembled him. When his memoirs were published, John figured that the Hatch regime would deny everything. But John had photos, videotapes, emails and other materials to document his story.

Chapter 45

Ice Cream? He had run out of options. He was broke and hungry. Ragged. There was only one place to which he could turn. Home. He had denounced his parents' values in recording after recording. But now they would have to shelter him so that he could straighten out the mix-up. Explain why his face had been rubbed the wrong way, but then as he entered the neighborhood where his parents lived, he was spotted as someone who fit the description of the man who murdered Ice Cream. Did he have it in for the whole family? A feud that didn't end with the murder of Ice Cream? He was spotted in a backyard of a middle-class garden, with plants that had been scrupulously pruned, all of the flower pots upright, the kind of middle middle-class stability that he ridiculed in his songs. Soon there were helicopters circling the neighborhood. Police cars were arriving. The 911s had gone off as soon as he entered the neighborhood. He made a run for it and found himself successfully standing in front of his parents' home. Before he could knock on the door, a shotgun blast blew his head off. There were demonstrations that evening against the latest stand-your-ground shooting.

But Mr. Rice was being hailed as a hero by others. In fact, Jesse Hatch invited him to be present in the gallery as his guest during the next State of the Union Speech. "Let that be a warning to other thugs and rapists who threaten our suburbs," Hatch said.

Under pressure, Jesse Hatch, left, and Clement Jones must explain why only Bob Krantz has ascended.

Chapter 46

The mood among those who were awaiting their Rapture had turned ugly. No one had been lifted into the clouds since Krantz's ascension. Crowds were demonstrating outside of the White House. Demanding their ascensions. People were tired of waiting to be whisked up. Chemical irritants were being sprayed on the crowds, and men on horseback were beating some with truncheons. Hatch and Clement had a press conference during which they demanded patience. It didn't work. Hatch, Clement and aides and cabinet officials fled Washington for Camp David. Because of the Rapture, Termite and his followers who had to go underground to avoid arrest orders became emboldened and emerged from their hideout in the woods of Oregon and held a press conference that held the Rapture to be a hoax created by the Deep State. If there wasn't enough chaos in Washington, when Jones, Hatch and party reached Camp David, they were informed that the head of the EPA, a coal baron, was found dead in one of his mansions. A note was left at his side. "It came between the planet and you. You lost." In order to deflect from the Rapture debacle, Rev. Clement Jones

with President Hatch standing next to him called for
an all-out manhunt for Boy Bishop, seen as a threat to
national security. Police Commissioner Brown read the
headlines about Boy Bishop's reappearance. A smile
crossed his lips.

Mayor Loathsome entered the diner where Brown
was waiting for him. Brown had already ordered a cup
of coffee. After removing his coat and hanging it on
a hanger, he slid into the booth, sitting across from
Brown. He slammed the newspaper onto the table.
"That son of a bitch Boy Bishop is now a loner."

"Easier to capture him," Brown said.

"Maybe you're right. But if I ever get my hands on
him, the first thing that I'm going to do is snip off those
blonde dread locks, fucking race traitor, I mean, excuse
me... I..."

"Skip it," Brown said. "It's cool." Larry's face turned
red, he was so embarrassed by the racist slip.

Outside they saw some Christmas carolers walking
by. They were ringing bells and singing. They held
posters aloft. But instead of the image of St. Nicholas,
there were images of Krampus, Black Peter's evil twin.
This was an ominous sign.

Chapter 47

The Devil was indistinguishable from the other passengers who boarded Delta for the one-way trip to Europe. He wore shades, a turtleneck sweater, slacks, and moccasins. He settled into his window seat. Soon they were flying over the Atlantic. He'd left America to return to where he'd fled when Christianity triumphed in Europe. Some of his copycats were left behind. A few had occupied the Vatican and were refusing to leave. Especially since a Black pope was threatening to move in. They saw themselves as protecting Western civilization. Now that he lacked his supernatural powers, he had to find a job like everybody else. Maybe he'd write a Netflix crime series. Like one of those set in Northern Europe. Nordic Noir. A small village. With a lake. And ice. A White girl has disappeared, the usual plot. He started to nod off. The shoreline of New York disappeared behind him. What would America do now? They wouldn't have the Devil to kick around anymore. Blaming their failures on him. Denouncing him. Lampooning him. Maybe they would grow up. Get over their Terrible Twos. Grow the fuck up. He was sitting in first class next to a blue-eyed blonde. He read her with the only paranormal gift that he still possessed. She was running off with some money after a bank embezzlement, leaving behind those with whom she was supposed to share it. The airline attendant came with the wine list. She was inspecting it. "May I recommend the Chablis?" the Devil asked.

Chapter 48

Rev. Clement Jones and his inner circle were having a conference, which, of course, excluded Hatch. Clement thought he knew Hatch's secret. If Clement didn't know his secret, (see *The Terrible 5s*), the only other person who knew his secret was his ex-wife, and Holly his favorite prostitute. He was subjected to endless embarrassments at the hands of Clement. Shame. Hatch spent hours alone in the vice president's mansion. Consigned to entertaining children and managing the Easter Egg roll. Now, the administration was in trouble. The Odin people led by Termite Control's RHAT TV spreading fanciful Earth 2 speculation. There were civil disturbances as the Odin people squared off with the Rapturists. Termite and his heavily armed escorts, *die kleinen Schwanzjungen*, were engaged in street battles.

Fights were occurring among family members over which members would ascend since after Bob Krantz, no one else had been Raptured. Clement placed another log on the fire located in the rustic Camp David cabin to which he had been assigned. There was a knock at the door. He opened the door.

Standing before him was John F. Kennedy Jr. and his wife, Carolyn. They were wearing rain gear, yellow coats and yellow hats. They were dripping wet even though it wasn't raining.

JFK Jr. said, "We need to talk."

The End

Ishmael Reed
January 3, 2021
Oakland, California
Year of the Plague

Questions that will be answered in *The Terrible Fives*

What advice did J.F.K. Jr. give to Jesse Hatch?

Will J.Q. take the job?

How will Rev. Clement Jones respond to the failed Rapture?

How will Miltiades II deal with the backlash over his marriage to Virginia Saturday?

Will the Devil get a job writing for Netflix?

Will Boy Bishop be captured?

What's in the package that Nance was supposed to deliver?

Will Black Peter return to fight his evil twin, Krampus?

Will Oswald Zumwalt, who rose to become head of North Pole Development Corporation, return? Imprisoned for accidentally killing Dean Clift's son while in school, he sat out *The Terrible Fours*. Will he return in *The Terrible Fives?*

And Vixen (*The Terrible Twos*). A former progressive who went over to the other side to become one of Termite's most ardent supporters, will she realize her dream? A White homeland in the state of Washington?

ALSO FROM BARAKA BOOKS

FICTION

Exile Blues by Douglas Gary Freeman

Things Worth Burying by Matt Mayr

Fog by Rana Bose

The Daughters' Story by Murielle Cyr

Yasmeen Haddad Loves Joanasi Maqaittik
by Carolyn Marie Souaid

NONFICTION

Stolen Motherhood, Surrogacy and Made-to-Order Children
Maria De Koninck

*Still Crying for Help, The Failure of Our
Mental Healthcare Services*
Sadia Messaili

A Distinct Alien Race, The Untold Story of Franco-Americans
David Vermette

*The Einstein File, The FBI's Secret War
on the World's Most Famous Scientist*
Fred Jerome

*Montreal, City of Secrets, Confederate Operations
in Montreal During the American Civil War*
Barry Sheehy

*Patriots, Traitors and Empires,
The Story of Korea's Struggle for Freedom*
Stephen Gowans

A People's History of Québec
Jacques Lacoursière and Robin Philpot

*The Question of Separatism, Quebec
and the Struggle Over Sovereignty*
Jane Jacobs